MY KIND OF SCHOOL

STORIES IN A CLASS OF THEIR OWN

MY KIND OF SCHOOL

STORIES IN A CLASS OF THEIR OWN

Edited by **Tony Bradman**

A & C Black • London

First published 2008 by
A & C Black Publishers Ltd
38 Soho Square, London, W1D 3HB

www.acblack.com

Collection copyright © 2008 Tony Bradman
Stories copyright © 2008 Alan Gibbons, Julia Green, Gus Grenfell,
Meg Harper, Francis McCrickard, Sophie McKenzie

The right of Tony Bradman to to be identified as the
editor of this work has been asserted by him in accordance
with the Copyrights, Designs and Patents Act 1988.

ISBN 978-0-7136-8506-0

A CIP catalogue for this book is available from the British Library.

This book is produced using paper that is made from wood
grown in managed, sustainable forests. It is natural, renewable
and recyclable. The logging and manufacturing processes conform
to the environmental regulations of the country of origin.

Printed and bound Great Britain by MPG Books Limited.

CONTENTS

INTRODUCTION
BY TONY BRADMAN

I often think you can tell what a school is like as soon as you walk through the door. That might be because I've visited lots of schools during my years as an author of children's books, and have acquired something of a feel for them. Some schools are nice and friendly and welcoming, while others are not quite such happy places. But whatever they're like, every time I go into one I feel myself slipping back through the years, and remembering my own school days.

There was the kindergarten in a hot foreign country where we had moved because of my dad's work. Family legend has it that I kept running away from that kindergarten, although no one seems to know why. There was the infants school I went to when we came back to London, the one with the dreadful yellow and blue uniform I hated. And there was the primary school in south London after that, the one where I got beaten up on my first day by a gang of wild boys. Strangely enough they became my best friends and, looking back, I now realise that for most of my time there I was very happy. I had a couple of great teachers, one of whom was called Mr Smith, who was a lot of fun and who read us *The Hobbit*, something which I think kick-started my interest in stories – which is probably how I ended up becoming a writer. Of course, there were still some things at school I didn't enjoy – cold swede and lumpy mashed potato for school dinners, compulsory swimming lessons at an old Victorian swimming baths – but I have a lot of very fond memories of Malcolm Primary. From there, I went on to a grammar school, and though I wouldn't say that school days were the best of my life, I did enjoy my time there, too.

So it's been more than interesting to put together this collection of stories about school life. Like me, most of us spend a large chunk of our early years at school, and it has a huge effect on us. Like Jack in Gus Grenfell's marvellous story *Dolphins* we might wonder how we're going to fit into a new and very different school. Sometimes our loyalties might be tested, as one boy discovers to his cost in *From The Ashes*, a gripping, hard-hitting story by Alan Gibbons. In Meg Harper's hilarious *Bonkers* another boy quickly finds out that school and friendships can be very complicated, while two girls from very different backgrounds help each other on a school trip in Francis McCrickard's poignant story, *The Residential*. Working out who your real friends are is the theme of Sophie McKenzie's great tale *The Lie*, and Julia Green follows a class through the last days of their primary school life in her fascinating story *One More Step*.

Like families, schools are all different and, at the same time, strangely the same. And somewhere in these pages you'll come across your kind of school – I can guarantee it!

DOLPHINS
BY GUS GRENFELL

The numbers he had written on the page stared up at Jack. At least *they* were reliable. *They* didn't change, unlike everything else in his life.

He was sitting at a table with a boy called Archie, who kept shooting glances at him, but Jack kept his head down.

"Where do you come from?" Archie asked.

"Does it matter?"

Archie was taken aback. "Sorry. Just trying to be friendly."

"Well, don't bother."

Miss McEwan, the class teacher, had said he would soon make friends, but Jack already had friends, even if they were hundreds of miles away. And he could still text and email them – when he could find service for his mobile; when they had an Internet connection in the wooden shack he was now supposed to call home. He had known they wouldn't go on living in the old house after Dad left, but why did they have to move to the back of beyond?

"We've just had a message." Miss McEwan didn't even have to raise her voice – there were only eleven in the class. "Fiona's rung from the post office. There's a school of dolphins on its way up the Sound. Shall we go and watch them?"

There was a buzz of excitement and everybody stopped what they were doing and made for the door.

Jack stayed where he was.

"Don't you want to see the dolphins, Jack?" Miss McEwan said as she walked past him. "They don't come very often, so it would be a pity to miss them."

Jack dragged himself to his feet and followed her out, across the road and onto the rocky shore where both classes of his new school were gathered.

"There they are!" Archie pointed, but Jack could only make out waves, until one leaped right out of the water.

"Did you see that?" Archie said. "Did you see how high it jumped? Kerpow!" He flung his arms in the air, scattering imaginary spray.

Miss McEwan took some photographs and handed the camera round. Jack shook his head when it was offered to him.

"They're only fish!" he said, unable to understand what all the fuss was about.

An older girl – Isabel, was it? – turned to him. "Dolphins aren't fish, they're mammals. Actually, they're very intelligent."

Was she trying to make him look stupid? Jack wasn't sure. He felt himself go hot, expecting everybody to look at him, but they were far more interested in watching the dolphins. He turned his back on them, and marched across the road to the school building, head down, hands in pockets.

Back in the classroom everyone was still full of it. Miss McEwan plugged the camera into a computer, and they all crowded round the screen to see the pictures they had just taken.

"That's a good one," Isabel said. It showed the lead dolphin leaping out of the water, and people watching from the shore. Jack was surprised to see himself there, too.

"Can we send it to the *Islander*, Miss?" Archie asked. "It'll make this week's edition if we email it today."

Jack couldn't believe that visiting dolphins were newsworthy enough to appear in the local paper. "Short of murders and armed robberies, are you?" he muttered, but either nobody heard, or they didn't think his remark was worth commenting on.

Jack didn't care; he wasn't part of their little world. He went back to the table and started writing numbers again – any numbers – digging his pencil into the paper until the lead broke.

Last night – the first in their new house – Jack had hardly slept. When friends in Leeds heard he was moving to an island off the west coast of Scotland, they'd said, "Ooh, it'll be so quiet." But it wasn't. He'd lain awake to the sound of waves crashing on the seashore and a shrieking wind rattling the roof slates. He didn't feel safe, and the total darkness made it even more scary.

In another way, of course, it *was* quiet. School had finished now, but Jack had nowhere to go, nothing to do and no mates nearby. Not even a dad to go home to anymore. And that morning he'd found out something that made it all worse. In England he'd been in Year 6, expecting to go to secondary school after the summer holidays, but the system in Scotland was different, and he'd be stuck in primary for another whole year.

At home, his kid sister was dancing round the kitchen. She was in the younger class, and he'd seen her at lunchtime, chatting, laughing and joining in games.

"Zoe's been telling me about the dolphins," Mum said. "It must have been exciting. And she's made so many friends already. Ben and I went for a walk up the glen, didn't we?" She turned to his little brother, who was kneeling on a chair at the table, hands covered in paint.

"We saw a stag," he said. "It had *big* horns." He banged his hands down on the paper in front of him and rubbed them round.

"And what are the horns called?"

Ben looked up and puzzled for a moment. "Antlers!"

"Good boy! You remembered."

Ben beamed, and gave his painting another smear.

Then Mum saw the scowl on Jack's face. "What's wrong, love?"

"I hate it here! I wish we'd stayed in Leeds."

Mum tried to put her arm round him, but Jack shrugged her off.

"I'm sure you'll like it when you get used to it," she said.

Jack didn't think he would. He crashed out of the kitchen, slamming the door behind him, stomped up the stairs to his little room under the roof and threw himself down on the bed.

Next morning, Jack's feelings hadn't changed. He trudged along the road to school, wishing Zoe wasn't so bright and cheerful. He felt like hitting her.

"Look!" she said, pointing to some black birds standing on a rock. "Cormorants."

"So?"

"You know, like we have on our school sweatshirts." She took the school crest between her fingers and displayed it proudly. Jack was about to slap her hand away, but she'd seen some of her classmates, and ran off to join them.

Jack's mood didn't improve in school. Miss McEwan was giving him lots of attention, finding out where he was up to, what he knew, what he was good at. With so few pupils, there was nowhere to hide.

He was sitting with Archie again. They were in the same year, and would move on together.

Archie wanted to talk to him about his family, where they lived, why they'd come to the island. Jack tried to ignore him, but Archie didn't give up.

"What's the matter?" he said. "Don't you like it here?"

"No. It's boring."

Archie looked surprised. "It must be better than living in a city full of noise, crowds, pollution, crime..."

That wasn't how Jack saw living in Leeds. It was the place he knew. His friends were there, the places he liked to go, the things he liked to do. But Mum had decided they needed a fresh start, somewhere completely different – the place she remembered from her childhood holidays.

"What was your old school like?" Archie asked.

"Better then this dump."

"Bigger, I suppose."

"Yeah. Two classes in each year. We had the best under-11 football team in Leeds."

You couldn't argue with that. Archie was impressed. "Were you in it?"

Jack frowned. "No. Why?"

"Just wondered. Not good enough, eh? Well, you can be in our team. Everybody is! We'll have a kick-around at break. Join in, if you want."

At his old school, Jack had never had a look in. Even the playground games were dominated by the big lads, and as for getting in the team... He'd been the smallest and youngest in his class, which didn't help.

When break came, Jack hung back. He wanted to play, but he didn't want them to think he was trying to be part of their group.

After a few minutes, Archie kicked the ball towards him. "Come on, Jack," he said.

Jack was tempted. He could feel himself being drawn into the game. He wanted to dribble the ball across the yard, or pass it to someone. Instead, he drew his foot back and hoofed the ball in the opposite direction. Archie put his hands on his hips and shook his head in bewilderment.

Miss McEwan was coming towards him now. Had she seen what he'd just done? Apparently not; she was all smiles. "I don't know whether Archie's mentioned it," she said, "but we go to the village hall after break, for country dancing."

"What?" Jack was appalled.

"Scottish country dancing. You'll soon pick it up. Then, when you go to dances at the hall, you'll know what to do. We call them ceilidhs. They're good exercise, too."

Jack couldn't imagine himself ever going to a ceilidh, and he certainly didn't want to dance.

In the hall, Miss McEwan was setting up a CD player. "Right," she said, when she was sure everyone was there. "We'll start with the *Gay Gordons*. Take your partners."

Jack stood with his back to the wall, glaring at anyone who looked as though they might want to dance with him, but Miss McEwan came and took his hand.

"I'll teach you the steps," she said. "You'll soon get the hang of it."

Things were going from bad to worse. He couldn't very well refuse, but his legs didn't want to move. Miss McEwan was stronger than she looked. She gripped his hand firmly, locked her other arm around his waist and dragged him stumbling across the floor until he had no option but to follow her lead.

Was this some strange kind of island punishment? He expected to be a laughing stock, but no one was taking any notice; it seemed to be perfectly acceptable that he was dancing with the teacher. He gave up resisting, and tried to work out where his feet were supposed to move – that way they were less likely to get trodden on.

"Well done!" Miss McEwan said at the end of the dance. "That was very good for a first time. You've got a great sense of rhythm."

Did she mean it? Jack wasn't sure. He almost felt pleased, but he certainly wasn't going to show it.

Nobody talked to him at lunchtime. Archie had given up trying to involve him in the football, and everybody else had their own friends and didn't want him hanging around, spoiling their fun. But that was all right. He didn't want to talk to them, either, and now they'd got the message.

Somebody rang a hand bell and Jack wandered back inside. There was a construction set on his table, and it was the same one he'd used at his old school. Jack enjoyed making things.

Miss McEwan said they were to work in pairs, but he didn't intend to work with Archie; he could make a perfectly good model on his own, so long as he had something to copy. There was a picture of a ferryboat on the wall. He sorted out the components he would need and set to work, ignoring everything else around him.

Half an hour later, he was finished, but Archie was having trouble with his model – it kept falling down. Archie banged the table and gave Jack a frustrated glance. "We're supposed to be working together," he said.

"Well, we're not, are we?" Jack felt smug. His model wasn't about to fall down. "What's it meant to be?" he asked.

Archie was wary. "It's... it's a dolphin-shaped spaceship."

Jack burst out laughing. "It'll never make the launching pad! What's this bit?" He pointed to a piece hanging off the side of Archie's tottering effort.

"Part of the dolphin design – a flipper. It's an array of solar panels to catch sunlight."

Jack shook his head. "Forget it, Archie, you haven't got a clue."

"All right!" Archie shouted. "See what you can do if you're so clever."

Jack leaned across the table, put in another connector below the flipper, and a couple of supporting rods. "There you go. Easy. Do you want me to fix the rest?"

Archie said nothing, and Jack turned his attention to the tail. Before long, Spaceship Dolphin was ready for liftoff.

Miss McEwan came to have a look. "That's great!" she said, ignoring Jack's model completely. "I'm glad you managed to work together. It's an exciting design – and very well built." She looked at Jack. "The details of this year's Tech Challenge have just arrived, and we need someone with your sort of skill. I think you and Archie could make the perfect team."

"Yes!" Archie quickly recovered his usual good humour. He put up his hand for a high five. "It means a trip to the mainland – we'll be representing the school – and the island!"

Jack ignored the hand. He was sure Miss McEwan had only said it to try and win him round – like saying he was good at dancing. Well, he wasn't going to get sucked in.

"I don't want to," he said. "It's not much to represent, is it? A stupid little school on a stupid little island."

There was a sudden silence; everyone looked at him.

"Maybe you're not ready for it yet," Miss McEwan said, struggling to keep her voice calm, but Jack could tell she was angry. Now she was against him, too. His resentment boiled over. He stood up, kicked his chair away, and brought his fist down on Spaceship Dolphin.

"I didn't want to come here in the first place!"

he yelled, and stormed out of the classroom. The last thing he saw was Archie looking dejectedly at the broken model.

Jack ran along the road, heading for home, looking back now and again to see if Miss McEwan – or somebody – was following him. But nobody was. It just proved they didn't care.

As he drew nearer to his house, he slowed down. If he appeared in the kitchen at this time, Mum would want to know why, and he didn't feel like talking to her just now. He needed to be alone.

Behind his house, a hill rose steeply, with a tree-lined stream – 'the burn' – tumbling down it. A sheep track snaked its way up, which would take him well away from the village. He started climbing, pushing himself as hard as he could, ignoring the ache in his legs and the fire in his lungs. He didn't stop until he reached a large, flat-topped rock about two-thirds of the way to the top. He hauled himself onto it, and lay there trembling and gasping for breath.

When the heaving in his chest subsided and his legs stopped shaking, he sat up, wrapped his arms round his knees and rested his head on them. He felt like running away, finding his way back to Leeds, where he belonged. But the only way off the island was by ferry, and it would be impossible to sneak on board without being seen.

His mobile beeped. Service at last! Now he'd be able to get his messages. Only one? He thumbed the 'read' button. It was from his gran, hoping he was 'settling in nicely' at his new school. There were none from his friends. Had they forgotten him already? He started writing a message to Dan, his best mate, but what was he going to say? 'Yesterday I saw some dolphins'? He wouldn't be very impressed; probably wouldn't even write back. Jack was a long way from Leeds, and not just in miles. Maybe he didn't belong there, either, any more.

A line of deer walked along the ridge above. A red squirrel scrambled through the branches of a tree by the burn, and below him in the bay the dolphins had swum into view again. These creatures belonged here. The rest of his class belonged here. For a moment Jack had an idea that maybe he would like to be part of it, too, instead of being the odd one out, the misfit, but he banished the thought. He didn't see how it could ever come about. He felt empty and hollow inside. What was he going to do?

He gazed across the Sound, to the long peninsula on the other side, then back again to the bay. It was calm and still, and he could see the dolphins clearly as they rose and fell in the water. But one of them was falling behind – it seemed to be caught in something. He wondered if the others would wait for it, or swim off and leave it, if it couldn't keep up.

Jack's eyes came back to the shore, to the village hall, the row of old fishermen's cottages and the school. It must be home time, because everybody was leaving. If he was quick, he could get to his house at the usual time and avoid awkward questions. He jumped off the rock and ran down the hill.

When he opened the kitchen door, Jack's heart sank. He'd seen that look on Mum's face before – half concerned, half angry – when he'd been in trouble.

"Miss McEwan tells me you ran out of school this afternoon."

So that was how she knew.

"Yes."

"Well?"

"Well what?"

"Why did you run off?"

"They all hate me there."

"I don't think they do, Jack. They're not sure about you yet. You haven't exactly gone out of your way to be liked, from what I hear."

Jack didn't want to listen to this. He made for the door, but Mum was too quick for him. She shut it and stood with her back against it. "Sit down, Jack. We need to talk."

Jack stood and glared at her, but he couldn't hold her gaze. He dropped his head and shambled over to the window seat.

"This can't go on," she said, moving to the stove to put the kettle on. "You can't spend the rest of your life being miserable. I know you miss your friends and everything in Leeds, but we're not going back there. This is where we live now, and you've got to make the most of it. It's a great place to be – the people are so friendly and they're genuinely pleased to have us in the village."

"That's what you think."

"It's true! Why don't you give them a chance to show it? Don't let the past drag you back and cut you off from everybody else. You're the one who'll suffer if you don't free yourself of it and make an effort to fit in."

"But I can't!" Jack was close to tears. What Mum said always sounded so reasonable – maybe it was, but that only made him feel worse. He'd already made things impossible for himself and he didn't know what he could do about it, even if he wanted to.

Before Mum could say any more, Zoe came running in with Ben. "Mum, Mum, the dolphins are in the bay again. One of them's all tangled up in something. Some people went out in a boat to try and help, but it wouldn't let them near."

"Dolphins. Splash!" Ben said, jumping up and down.

"Don't worry." Mum wanted to sound reassuring. "It may free itself."

Zoe looked at her, wide-eyed and anxious. "But what if it can't?"

"Well..." Mum paused for a moment, and looked at Jack. "We'll have to wait and see."

In Leeds, Jack knew people who had been transferred from one school to another because they weren't happy at the first one, but here he didn't have the choice. He thought of asking Mum in the morning if she'd say he was ill and keep him off, but he knew she wouldn't.

What would happen when he walked into the classroom? He was dreading it, but Miss McEwan went through the normal routine as though nothing had happened. She said, "Good morning, Jack," and smiled at him – but he knew how she really felt. She must be biding her time. The rest of the class just got on with their work, though Jack caught people giving him a quick look now and again, and Archie wasn't his usual talkative self. Jack didn't feel comfortable.

They hadn't been working long, when the secretary appeared from the office. "The dolphins are coming back down the Sound," she told Miss McEwan. "One of them's struggling, apparently, and the coastguards are there – they want to try and catch it beside the cleit." That was a long tongue of rock that stuck out into the sea opposite the school.

Jack didn't hang back this time – anything to get out of the classroom; and he was curious to know what the coastguards would do. Outside, he could see a rigid inflatable boat with several figures clad in yellow oilskins and life jackets. There were two local boats, too, and they were gently shepherding the dolphins down the coast, as near to the shore as they could. The dolphins didn't show any signs of wanting to break away, and the struggling one was definitely going slower than it had been the last time he saw it.

Jack ran along the cleit, and Archie followed. "Don't go too far," Miss McEwan called. "You don't want to scare them."

They stopped, and watched as the boats ushered the dolphins nearer. As they grew closer to the cleit, the lead dolphin altered course to head into open water, with the others following.

"Let them go," one of the coastguards shouted, and they brought the nose of the lifeboat round to cut off the injured one that was lagging behind.

The dolphin seemed to be exhausted and disorientated, floundering in the shallower water. It was unable to make a break for it and follow the others.

Jack expected it to stop when it became aware of the rocks, but it kept on coming, heading straight for where he and Archie were standing. Suddenly, he realised that it didn't have enough room to turn and it was going to crash into the cleit. Without thinking, Jack jumped into the water. Better it should crash into him than hurt itself more on the rocks. Jack gasped at the cold, and braced himself, holding his hands out to cushion the blow. At the last moment, the dophin turned aside, though not quickly enough to avoid contact. It brushed against Jack, knocking him off his feet in the chest-high water. He let his legs float up, and trod water beside the dolphin as the coastguard cut the outboard motor and let the lifeboat drift in front of them.

At last, the dolphin became still. It seemed to know that there was no escape now, and maybe it even understood that it wasn't in danger.

Jack could see what the trouble was. "It's caught in an old piece of net," he said. "A flipper's gone through the mesh and it's digging into the flesh on top."

"Stay there," the coastguard said. "It seems to trust you."

One of the others climbed out of the boat and came round to Jack's side. Jack had his arm across the dolphin's back, willing it to stay still. He could feel it trembling while the man found a spot where he could slide his knife under the tight polypropylene. He sawed it back and forth until the last strands gave way. Jack pulled the net off, leaving the dolphin free at last.

The boat moved off, and Jack scrambled back onto the cleit. To his amazement, everybody was clapping and cheering.

"I'll put you in my incident report," the coastguard said as he started the lifeboat's motor. "You're from the new family, aren't you?"

"Well done, Jack!" Miss McEwan was coming over the rocks to congratulate him, and this time he knew she meant it.

"We've got loads of photos," Archie said, grinning from ear to ear. "This could make the front page of the *Islander*. They love a rescue story. I can see the headline now: 'Local Hero Saves Dolphin'."

Local hero? That wasn't how Jack thought of himself; he was sure that Archie or one of the others would have done the same thing. Still, he couldn't help enjoying his unexpected popularity.

The rescued dolphin stayed motionless for a short while. Then, slowly at first but gaining in confidence, it swam out to where the others were waiting for it. Jack was glad he had helped to set it free. People turned away and drifted back to school.

It was break. Archie retrieved his football from a corner of the playground and threw it in the air. Jack hesitated for a moment; something inside him still wanted to ignore it, but he pushed the feeling away and rose to meet the ball.

"Good one!" Archie said, heading it back again.

Jack took the ball on his knee, bounced it to the other and smashed it against the school wall with a powerful kick.

"Go-o-o-al!" Archie shouted, raising his hands in the air.

Jack turned away for a moment. He could still see the dolphins, but they were all together now; there wasn't one hanging back. The first dolphin leaped out of the water and led them away, down the Sound towards the open sea.

FROM THE ASHES
BY ALAN GIBBONS

Liam's the one who broke the news, which makes sense knowing what I do now.

"You're not going to believe it," he said, bursting through the door. "Oakwood burned down last night. It's completely gutted."

Liam's our Jack's best mate. I remember the way he looked that Monday morning. He was flushed, eyes wide and bright, as if he was reporting on the result of a footy match, not the school burning down. I didn't think anything of it at the time. People get excited about stuff like that. It's only human.

Immediately, Mum walked in from the kitchen. "What was that, Liam?" she asked, wiping her hands on a tea towel.

"It's the school," Liam told her, confirming his story, "it got burned down overnight."

"Oakwood?"

Liam nodded. "Yes."

Mum turned her eyes on Jack. There was something strange about the way he was behaving. He was like a kind of ghost hovering at the edge of things. Liam was doing all the talking, as usual. Jack just looked on. That's their friendship. Liam leads. Jack follows.

"Go tell your dad," said Mum.

But Dad was already on his way back into the house. He'd been loading the car ready to go to work. He barged past Jack as if he wasn't there. One of the neighbours must have broken the news. His eyes were bulging, his face red, the skin tight over his cheeks. Dad didn't usually get angry. I just stared. So did my little sister Ruby. We weren't used to seeing him like that.

"Pass me the phone," he said, eyes hard with shock. "I've got to call work and tell them I'll be in late. I'm going to go down to the school. Does anybody want to come?"

Dad was Chair of Governors at Oakwood. He was so proud when he got the job a month earlier. Now he was devastated, like the building. *His* school. Destroyed. "Maybe it's not as bad as people are making out," he said, but I didn't hear any hope in his voice.

Oakwood looked much worse than we'd imagined. The school's only five minutes walk from our house. The moment we stepped out of the front door we could smell the acrid reek of burning in the air. Mum said later that she'd smelled it while she was making breakfast, but it was early November so she thought it had something to do with Bonfire Night.

The scene in Oakwood Drive was like one of those old photos from the Blitz. We'd just done World War II in class so the images were fresh in our minds. The school building was a blackened shell. Fire engines were drawn up around it and the firefighters were still dousing down the embers. Plumes of thin, grey smoke were rising into a purple, stormy sky. Here and there, knots of parents and kids were standing around, looking on. One or two of the kids were in school uniform, but there would be no lessons that day.

Ruby stared at the devastation. "I made a Chinese lantern," she said. She was really proud of it. Now it was destroyed, reduced to ashes. She burst into tears.

Dad picked out Mrs Glover and went across to talk to her. Hearing Dad's tread on the drenched, sooty ground, she turned and gave him a thin smile. They talked for a few minutes, shaking their heads and glancing over. I remember this little girl out of Reception coming up to Mrs Glover and slipping her hand into the head teacher's. Mrs Glover knelt down and gave the kid a hug. It seemed to sum up the way people were feeling. Soon, Dad was back.

"The fire started in the early hours of the morning," he reported. "They set light to two classrooms. It was deliberate."

Then he made a comment about the people who did it. He swore. That's another thing he didn't usually do. Loads of weird stuff was happening. I don't know why, but it felt as if the earth was shifting under my feet. I saw Dad frown when he noticed that Jack was there.

"What are you doing still hanging round here, son?" he said, glancing at his watch. "The Comp's still standing. You'd better get off to school."

Jack nodded and left with Liam. Even then, I had a feeling something was wrong.

That afternoon some of the lads in our class went down to the rec on Rose Lane to play football. Jermaine called for me. He's my best mate. His nickname is Germ, as in germ warfare. We felt bad about what had happened, but there was nothing we could do so we took advantage of the unofficial holiday. The news said we'd be off for the rest of the week while arrangements were made for us to be taught elsewhere.

"Have you heard the rumours?" Germ asked when we took a break.

"What rumours?"

Germ took a swig from a can of Coke. "They say it was somebody from the High School," he answered. "Some lads out of Year 9 did it."

There was a knot in my stomach. Year 9! Barely formed thoughts were floating round the back of my mind. Sometimes, for no real reason at all, you know something in your water even before there's any proof.

"I mean, this is heavy duty," Germ said. "Arson's serious."

Tell me something I don't know, I thought. I remembered the eager, wide-eyed way Liam broke the news about the fire and the way our Jack had stood just behind him, kind of pale and uneasy. No, it couldn't be. Jack had a wild streak but no way would he be that stupid.

"Has anybody said a name?" I asked.

Germ shook his head. "Not that I know, but

it's bound to come out. Everybody knows everybody on this estate."

Everybody knows everybody. He was right there.

Jack was home by the time I got back. Ruby skipped ahead of me and said hi to him. The High School finishes at three o'clock. He was standing in the kitchen, drinking milk straight from the carton. He had his tie knotted halfway down his chest. Lots of the kids do that. It's a way of wearing the uniform but not wearing it, if you get my drift. If Mum and Dad catch him with it pulled down low like that, they go ballistic, say it's disrespectful. Same with drinking straight from the milk carton.

"Don't let Mum catch you doing that," I told him. "You're supposed to pour it into a glass."

"And you're supposed to mind your own business," Jack retorted.

He saw the way Ruby and I were looking at him.

"Sorry," he said. "I didn't mean to snap."

I shrugged. "It's no skin off my nose."

We stood looking at each other. It's funny the way you do that sometimes. There are no words, but the way you hold yourself, the way you stare somebody out, it says more than words. Some of the files Dad had as School Governor were on the table. I glanced at the files, then at Jack. Jack dropped his eyes and turned to go.

"Are you OK?" I asked.

By then, Jack had his back to me.

"Sure," he said, without turning round. "Why shouldn't I be?"

Ask him, I told myself. Ask him straight out. Did you have something to do with the fire? But I couldn't find the words. I suppose I was willing it not to be true. Maybe, if I wished it hard enough, the bad thoughts would go away. Then everything would be all right. Jack had reached the doorway by then.

"Jack," I said, still trying to pluck up the courage.

"Yes?"

"You take care, yeah?"

It was a weird thing to say. I was in Year 6, 11 years old. He was 14. Isn't *he* the one who's supposed to say all the big brother stuff to *me*? Somehow, it's never worked out that way. Jack's always acted younger than his age. He half-turned. He gave me the longest look then carried on into the hallway. He didn't say anything at all. A moment later, the front door slammed.

On the Thursday evening there was a meeting at English Martyrs church hall for all the Oakwood parents. Mum asked Jack to baby-sit me and Ruby. Some baby-sitter he was. He just stayed in his room playing on the PS2. I was the one who answered the phone calls and kept an eye on Ruby and got her a drink and a snack. I love Jack to bits but he makes me really angry sometimes. He lives in his own little world. I did my homework. Ruby had all her toys laid out on the living room floor.

The minutes ticked by. It was a long meeting. There had been all kinds of rumours. Some people said we were going to be taught in spare classrooms at the High School. Others said we were going to share with English Martyrs school up the road. I didn't like the sound of that. Sometimes there had been fights between kids from Oakwood and English Martyrs. I wasn't sure how well we would mix. About eight o'clock the door bell rang. Ruby raced down the hall.

"Mum, Dad," she squealed.

It wasn't them. When Ruby managed to get the door open, there was Liam standing on the step.

"Is Jack in?" he asked.

I stepped back to let him enter.

"He's upstairs," I said.

I watched Liam climb the stairs. Was that tobacco smoke I smelled on his jacket? Liam thought he was the big man, really streetwise, and our Jack was stupid enough to fall for it. Disappointed, Ruby went back into the living room. I stayed at the bottom of the stairs, trying to make sense of the rumble of conversation upstairs in Jack's room. I'd been there no more than a couple of minutes when I heard Jack shouting. Seconds later, Liam came running down the stairs, red-faced and angry. He rushed straight past me and threw the door open, disappearing into the night. Suddenly I had this big lump in my throat. I'd been trying not to believe my suspicions. But now...? I shot a glance upstairs and there was Jack, staring after him. I elbowed the front door shut and caught Jack's eye.

"What was all that about?" I demanded.

"Nothing."

I flicked a glance at Ruby to make sure she wasn't listening, then climbed the stairs. I felt as if, any moment, they would give way under me and drop me into a black hole.

"Talk to me, Jack," I said. "I know something's going on."

Jack looked scared. It was enough to make a prickle run the length of my spine.

"Come in here," Jack said.

I followed him into his room. The light was switched off. The PS2 war game washed the walls with its flickering colours.

"I was there," Jack said, "when the school burned down."

When he spoke, there was a quiver in his voice he couldn't disguise. I stood looking at him, a chill creeping through my veins. I suppose I'd always known but it didn't make finding out any easier.

"You idiot," I said finally.

Then a thought occurred to me.

"But how could you have been there?" I asked. "Oakwood burned down in the early hours of the morning. That's what the news said."

"I was sleeping over at Liam's," Jack reminded me. "We sneaked out of the house about midnight. His parents were already asleep in bed. We met up with some of his mates, older lads. I didn't know what they were going to do. I didn't want anything to happen. I just..."

"You just went along with it," I interrupted.

Jack nodded. "I didn't mean it to happen. You have to believe me. It all got out of hand."

His eyes were darting nervously towards the door as if he half expected somebody to be eavesdropping. I must have still looked confused because he filled in the rest of the details.

"Mum and Dad let me stay over at Liam's that night," Jack said. "Do you remember? They thought we were doing revision."

"And you went over to Oakwood and broke in?" I asked. "You're crazy."

Jack lowered his eyes. "I know." He ran his hands through his hair. "I swear, I didn't set any fires. I didn't even go inside. I just watched."

The moment he said it, I knew he was telling the truth. I love him and I know he wouldn't choose to do anything bad.

"But you did nothing to stop them?" I asked.

That was Jack. Weak. He just had to go along with things.

He shook his head. "If I'd known what Liam and the others had planned..." His voice trailed off. "What do I do?" he asked. "What the hell do I do?"

And what do I do? I wondered. What's the right thing?

Dad went through what had been discussed with Ruby and me when he got in from the meeting. Ruby's in Year 3 so it concerned her, too.

"Neither the High School nor English Martyrs have enough room for everybody," Dad said. "There was some talk of splitting the kids up, sending half to the High School and half to English Martyrs. I argued against it. Once you start splitting up the school, it ceases to exist as a community. I said Oakwood had to rise like a phoenix from the ashes."

Mum smiled. "Your dad made a really good speech. He made the councillors listen. Now he thinks he's Martin Luther King."

Dad rolled his eyes but he was obviously pleased with himself. "So here's what's going to happen. Do you remember West Park school?"

I just looked at him. I couldn't think straight. I was haunted by what Jack had just told me. But I forced out the words. "The one that closed down?" I said. "Yes."

"Well," Dad said, "it closed because of falling numbers. The building isn't in bad shape and it's only a mile away. We're going to move Oakwood there. Work starts tomorrow. We can be in within a matter of weeks."

Ruby was excited. She was missing school. Jack would have said she was weird but I knew what she meant. You always say you hate school but I felt the same way she did. Then I thought about what would happen if the truth came out. What if people found out what Jack had done? I was about to go back to my homework when Dad dropped his bombshell.

"Oh," he said, "there's one bit of good news."

I asked a question with my eyes.

"The police have got one of the youths who started the fire," Dad said. "He's bound to grass on the others."

That's when I knew what I had to do.

"There's something you've got to know," I said. "Wait there."

I went for Jack. When he followed me into the living room, Mum and Dad swapped puzzled glances.

"Tell them," I said, pushing Jack forward. "If you don't, I will."

Finding it hard to face them, he began his tale.

Dad resigned as Chair of Governors the next day. I've never seen him so angry or so upset. It was as if he was carrying the whole world on his shoulders. He had a day off work and took Jack down to the police station to confess. The next week was terrible. For starters, we had to let the family know what Jack had done. Then I told Germ. At first, his parents wouldn't let him play out with me. It was the same for Ruby. She was heartbroken. She didn't know why she couldn't see her friends. Then there was the way the neighbours looked at us. What were we supposed to do? Say sorry for existing? It wasn't me that burned Oakwood down, or Ruby or Mum or Dad. It wasn't even Jack really. But for a week or two, we were all made to feel guilty. People who used to smile and say hello looked the other way. Jack had made us feel like rubbish.

Then, slowly, it started to get better. Mum went to see Germ's parents and the parents of Ruby's friends. She wouldn't talk about it when she got back but, after a few days, Germ came round. The next day one of Ruby's friends invited her to a birthday party. I can't say it's something I'd like to go through again. Your stomach turns over every time you meet somebody. But we came out the other side.

Every evening, Dad went to the new school and took Jack with him. Nobody worked harder to get it ready. They helped with the new furniture. They carried in all the teachers' stuff in cardboard boxes. A couple of times I went with them. It was really strange. People talked to you, but there was something in their voice, as if they were talking over a wall.

I actually felt sorry for Jack, even though he was the one who made things bad for us all. He went round with his eyes looking down at the floor. Everybody was talking about him. Sometimes they didn't even make any effort to keep their voices down. I could see him flinch as he overheard them. He also lost all his friends, if that's what you can call them. The first lad the police arrested kept his mouth shut. It was Jack's statement that put Liam and the others in the frame. They wrote Jack's name on walls all round the estate.

Jack Mooney = Grass, that's what the slogans said. Some friends! But my stupid brother had finally done the right thing and that's all that mattered.

Then, one crisp, cold morning it was time to go back to school. We walked past the old school on the way to the new site. They'd just started clearing it. There were workmen and JCBs moving rubble. When we reached the gates of the new school we lined up in our classes. Mrs Glover made a short speech.

"Sometimes there are challenges in life," she said. "Things don't always go the way you expect. Several weeks ago, some boys burned down our school."

I knew people were looking at me, but I stared straight ahead. I knew Ruby was doing the same. She's so little, but she's stronger than you'd think. Mum and Dad had told us what to do.

"But we can't keep looking back," Mrs Glover said. "The boys who did it will be punished. They must learn from their mistakes. It is now up to all of us to make the new Oakwood even better than the old one." She pointed to the entrance. "A lot of people have worked hard to get the building ready for us. That includes one of the boys who was there when the fire happened."

I tensed. She meant Jack.

"It takes courage to admit your mistakes and put them right," she said. "Now your teachers are going to lead you inside one class at a time. It's a new start."

When it was Year 6's turn we walked through the new reception area and into class. There was a mat in the entrance and a shield over it. Both read: "This is Oakwood".

The police have cautioned Jack. We're still waiting to hear what they're going to do to the others. Mrs Glover phoned Dad yesterday. She doesn't want him to resign as Chair of Governors. Dad says he's going to think about it. It's a tough call. All I know, it isn't just Oakwood that's putting itself back together. It's our family, too. We're trying to help Jack start over. Like that phoenix, we're rising. From the ashes.

BONKERS
BY MEG HARPER

"Twenty-four, twenty-five, twenty-six... How many do you make it, Mrs Alcock?" asked Miss Newlands, looking anxious.

"Oh no... Not already," I heard Mr Burn mutter under his breath. "I don't believe it."

"Twenty-six," said Mrs Alcock. "There's one missing. Stand still, everyone. We need to count again."

"Please, Miss..." I said, sticking up my hand. "It's probably..."

"Not now, Damien," said Mrs Alcock, "I'm trying to count."

"But, Miss..." It was hopeless. The three teachers and the three parent helpers were all mouthing numbers, their heads waggling like a row of startled chickens. Mrs Alcock was Queen Hen with her huge twitchy bottom, fat wobbly arms, beady little eyes and sharp red mouth.

It was the day of the grand opening ceremony for the brand-new, state-of-the-art theatre, which has been built at our school, and the place was heaving. The Lower School Drama Group, the Upper School Drama Group, the GCSE Drama Group – well, every drama group the school could boast – we were all going to put on a performance. I've never seen so many stressed-out teachers in my life. There was even this dead-famous actor coming (not that I've ever heard of him). But most of the female teachers seemed to think he was at least as hot as Johnny Depp.

"Do you really think that actor bloke will come?" said Mannie, who was standing next to me. Even though he's got a reputation for being a bit wild at school, he's easily impressed. "D'you think he'll watch *all* our performances?"

"Course. And don't worry, you'll be great," I said. Mannie looked green with nerves. He had a leading role in our play. "Though I'm more bothered about Nick right now," I added. "He's disappeared."

"Oh no," said Mannie. "Not now! Have you told Miss?"

"I tried," I said. "But she wouldn't listen. Too busy counting."

"She still is," said Mannie.

"They all are," I said, and sat down in disgust.

"Twenty-six, no, twenty-seven – that's right! Nassar, did you move? Stay still, will you! Eleven, twelve, thirteen... How many did you say we should have, Mrs Alcock?"

Six adults, all counting and all getting different numbers. We could be here for ever. I sidled up to Miss Newlands (she's young and pretty and most of us lads have got the hots for her, including Mr Burn) and tugged at her sleeve.

"Miss, it's Nick," I said. "He went off exploring, I think."

"What? Oh good grief, why didn't you tell me before?" she gasped. "He could be anywhere by now!"

I shrugged. "He's only been gone five minutes," I said. "And I did try..."

But she wasn't listening, she was telling the Queen Hen.

"Damien!" Squawk, squawk. "Why didn't you say so at once?"

"I tried to..." I muttered, but I knew it wasn't worth the effort. Suddenly, all the hens were clucking and flapping and then Mr Burns (token rooster) was sent off to see if he could find Nick.

We, meanwhile, got forced into line and cackled at for a bit – didn't we know we must all stay together, mustn't wander off, keep in sight of a teacher or a parent AT ALL TIMES (big squawk for that bit), this is a big occasion, etc., etc.

Well, yes, we did, actually. We weren't the ones who'd gone off exploring.

"I know I shouldn't say this," I said to Mannie, "'cos Nick really loves drama – but sometimes I just wish he didn't!"

Mannie nodded glumly. The three of us had been friends since infant school. We were used to Nick's slightly unusual ways. *We* knew how to handle him. But sometimes he could be a real pain.

Anyway, we waited patiently (well, *we* thought we were patient even if the Queen Hen didn't!) and had a good laugh at the kids in stupid costumes. At least the Queen Hen had chosen a play in which we could wear our own clothes.

"I don't want any fuss about costumes," she had said. "Your parents are quite busy enough. My mother has never let me forget the time I had to play the part of the Christmas Fairy and the hours she spent making my dress." She paused. "And why is that so funny, Damien Milbank? Something hilarious about that, is there?"

"No, Miss, sorry, Miss," I spluttered, desperately trying to wipe a picture of the Queen Hen wearing an enormous tutu from my mind.

We'd shuffled our way into one of the drama studio suites by the time Mr Burn returned with Nick. Mr Burn was hot and red and clawing Nick's shoulders; Nick looked as happy as a lark. I thought the Queen Hen might peck him to death, but she satisfied herself with a good, long squawk and then Nick came bounding over to Mannie and me.

"You'll never guess what I found," he gasped. "There's this ladder fixed to the wall and when you go up you can get onto this huge, strong mesh thing that goes right across the top of the stage. And there was a bloke walking on it, fixing lights that hung underneath. It's amazing. But Mr Burn didn't seem interested – just cross." Nick looked puzzled, the way he generally does when he's in trouble. Because Nick never means to be difficult – his brain just isn't wired the way teachers expect it to be. I mean, I'm sure Nick knows he isn't supposed to wander off as a general rule – it's just that if he sees something worth wandering off for, it genuinely never occurs to him that he shouldn't.

"Nick," I said. "There's masses of exciting stuff in this theatre – but you've got to stay with us, OK? Stick with Mannie and me. Don't go walkabout, OK? You could get seriously lost. Do you understand?"

"Yeah," he said, "I know. But you should see that mesh thing. It's like a giant trampoline. I'd just love to be that man, fiddling with the lights."

"No, Nick!" I said, grabbing his arm. "Don't even think about it, all right?"

Just at that moment, one of the parent helpers came hurrying up.

"Hi, you three," she said. "I'm Jessica Laing's mum. I'm keeping an eye on you tonight, OK? Now, Nick, you know you're not to wander off, don't you?"

I weighed up Mrs Laing. She looked sweet and innocent and a lot like Jessica, who is also sweet and innocent and would never dream of wandering off, climbing up strange ladders or doing anything other than paying attention to the teacher and doing her work properly. Mrs Laing smiled her lovely Jessica smile, full of warmth and enthusiasm and ignorance about Nick. I shook my head and sighed. *Bonkers*, I thought.

Fortunately, after we'd all crammed into the main theatre for a 'briefing', we didn't have long to wait before we were told it was time to warm up – the audience was arriving. Then disaster struck.

"I don't feel very well," Mannie suddenly said to Mrs Laing. "I feel sick."

"Oh dear," she said. "It's very warm in here – maybe it's that. Would you like some water?"

"No, thank you," said Mannie. "I think I need to go to the toilet."

"It's probably just nerves," said Mrs Laing. "You'll feel much better once you've got started."

Mannie rolled his eyes and looked pained.

"Perhaps you should sit down and take a few deep breaths," said Mrs Laing.

I looked at Mannie's face, which is usually a nice warm shade of brown. It had gone sort of slime-coloured and he was whitish around his mouth.

"Maybe I should just take him to the loo?" I said.

"Oh no, dear. We can't have the two of you going off on your own. I'll have a word with Mrs Alcock and see what she thinks."

Bonkers, I thought, watching her pushing her way anxiously through the crowd of kids.

"You are seriously going to puke, aren't you?" I said.

Mannie groaned and clutched his stomach. "And the other," he said.

"Come on," I said. "We can't wait around here. There must be a loo somewhere. Can you run?"

"Not sure."

"Well, try!"

I turned to the bunch of giggling girls who were warming up beside us – if you can call sticking out your chest and wiggling your hips warming up.

"Look, don't let Nick wander off, OK?" I said. "I've got to take Mannie to the loo."

"OK, Damien," cooed the biggest and silliest of the girls, giving me The Look. (I can't stand The Look. What it means is "I fancy you but I'm too stupid / silly / scared to tell you so can you please just notice how cute I am?" Of course, I never get The Look from anyone worth getting it from. Not Miss Newlands, for example. Not Jessica Laing. Sensible girls don't do The Look.)

I ran after Mannie, who was stumbling through the crowd, clutching his tummy. *Doesn't look good*, I thought. *Doesn't look good at all*!

"Hey, you!" shouted a big, burly teacher voice. "No running!"

"My friend's..." I tried to explain.

"Didn't you listen to the briefing?"

"I know, but my friend's..."

At that moment, we both heard the unmistakable whoops and splat of stomach contents hitting the floor. Mannie hadn't made it in time. I decided that wasn't my problem.

"I'd better get Mrs Alcock," I said and left the teacher to deal with the Mannie mess.

Queen Hen was fuming and flapping like she'd got several eggs stuck. When she caught sight of me, she rushed over as if I was a worm she was about to squidge for her dinner. Mrs Laing came running after her, wringing her hands. Fleetingly, I wished she was Jessica – then if she had burst into tears I could have done something manly like getting her a tissue. But Jessica was nowhere in sight so I just braced myself for the attack.

"And where do you think you've been?" demanded the Queen Hen. "Where's Manjit? And where's Nick?"

I groaned and turned to glare at the Giggling Gits. The big one shrugged and gave me The Look again. The Look! When she'd let Nick disappear!

Beyond bonkers!

"Mannie's been sick in the corridor," I said.

"Manjit? Sick? But he's our leading man!" The Queen Hen looked as horrified as if her beak had just dropped off.

"Well, Mrs Laing thought it was nerves. He might be all right now."

"Let's hope so," flapped the Queen Hen. "But where's Nick?"

"I don't know," I said. "He must have gone when I went with Mannie." I felt worn out already and the performance hadn't even started.

Mrs Laing was looking distinctly tearful now. "I'm so sorry," she kept saying. "I couldn't think what to do!"

Tiredly, I rooted in my pocket and pulled out a tissue wrapped round some old chewing gum. Mrs Laing didn't seem to mind. She wiped her eyes gratefully and I imagined she was Jessica.

The Queen Hen was still flapping. Should she go and sort out Mannie? Should she go and look for Nick? One of them had to stay with the group – but two children were missing. What was the best thing to do?

"Maybe Mrs Laing could go to look after Mannie and ask them to put a message on the

PA for Nick?" I said. "Then you could stay here?'

The Queen Hen looked down at me in surprise and all her feathers (I know she doesn't really have feathers, but you get the picture) seemed to settle.

"What a good idea, Damien!" she said and then, in case I got too pleased with myself. "For once!"

But just then, Mrs Laing gave a little gasp of delight. "Here's Nick. Thank goodness for that!"

"Where?" said the Queen Hen.

I sighed. "Just came in through the door, Miss. Nick! Over here!"

Nick turned towards us as if in a dream. I shouted again. I knew he was in a world of his own, a world of whatever technical wonders he had discovered in the theatre.

He came over, smiling a dazed smile.

"Nick!" squawked the Queen Hen. "How many times do I have to tell you NOT TO WANDER OFF?"

"Cluck, cluck, cluck," agreed Jessica's mum.

I tried not to think about Jessica. It was no fun watching her mum behave like an idiot.

"Sorry, Miss," Nick said, as if waking from a dream. "It's a fantastic place this, isn't it?"

The Queen Hen seemed to slump. "Did you hear

any of that, Nick?" she demanded. You could tell she was thinking what a long evening it was going to be. Silly woman. Quite bonkers. She ought to be used to Nick by now.

After that, things seemed to settle down. Mannie was returned by the burly teacher, looking surprisingly healthy. "Think I ate too many sweets after tea," he said. "I'll be fine now."

The show had started, so we had to hang around waiting for our call. We were supposed to run through our lines and warm up our voices but it was pretty boring after a while. Then Mannie did his frog with bellyache impression again. I've never seen anyone go quite so green.

"Mrs Alcock!" I yelled. "Mannie's going to be..."

Whoops! Too late. Again.

"Why didn't he say he was still feeling ill?" the Queen Hen clucked at me. "Why didn't you tell me?"

"But, Miss, I didn't..."

It was hopeless. She never listens. Too busy squawking.

"Urgh, Miss, it stinks in here. Urgh, Miss..." everyone started complaining.

"Quiet!" squawked the Queen Hen. Everyone

fell silent under her beady gaze. We knew that deadly change of tone. One peck and instant death. No one moved.

"Mr Burn, if you wouldn't mind...?" she said, regally indicating the splat on the floor. (*Typical! The token rooster gets the worst job*, I thought.) "And Miss Newlands, perhaps you could find a quiet place where Manjit could lie down?"

Mr Burn didn't look too impressed with the task he'd been given but didn't dare argue.

The Queen Hen drew herself up to her full height and fixed us with her killer eye. "It's quite clear," she said, "that Manjit is not going to be able to perform tonight. So we must find someone else to take his role. Hmm..." Her gaze swept the room and we all tried to hide behind one another. "Damien – yes, you'll do. Perfect!"

"Me, Miss?" I said. "Perfect?" (*Bonkers*, I thought. *Stark staring bonkers*!)

"Perfect because the part you have now is tiny and will hardly be missed. And despite your frequently deplorable behaviour, you have a sharp mind and probably know Manjit's lines."

It was true. I did. In fact, if it wasn't for me going over them with him a million times, Mannie would never have learnt them.

"Stop staring at me like a miserable worm!" the Queen Hen continued. "And go and run through it all with Jessica."

Jessica. In the play, Jessica was this awful bully who made Mannie's life a misery. She's a brilliant actor. The thought of trying to match up to her made me feel as sick as Mannie. I gulped.

"Er... Miss. I don't think I can do it," I said, pathetically. "Pick someone else. Please!"

"You'll be fine, Damien," said Jessica, suddenly appearing at my elbow. "Come on, we haven't much time."

So that was that. We had about 40 minutes before we were due to go on and I had to spend all of them with Jessica Laing. It would have been bliss but for the performance at the end – and the appalling thought that I might let her down big time!

But Jessica seemed completely unfazed.

"This way," she said and steered me down the corridor. She was certainly more decisive than her mum!

"Where are we going?" I asked.

"In here. I found it when we were looking for Nick." She pushed open a big door and flicked on the lights. We were standing in a workshop.

"Nowhere else is free," she said, "and we need to be somewhere quiet on our own."

I gulped. My legs seemed to have turned to jelly.

"Well?" she said. "Are you OK to start? You *do* know most of Mannie's lines, don't you?"

"Yes," I said, faintly. Then, getting a grip on myself, "Yes, of course I do. It was *me* that made him learn them."

Jessica grinned. "I thought you might have done," she said. "Right – from where I come in then. Ready?"

I took a deep breath. "Ready," I said.

At last it was time for us to go and wait backstage for our performance to start. Queen Hen couldn't resist a quick squawk as I trooped past.

"I'm relying on you, Damien," she clucked. "See if you can impress me – for once!"

Great – I thought teachers were meant to be encouraging!

Jessica gave me a cheery smile. "You'll be fine," she said. "Stop worrying."

My stomach gave a giant lurch. It was nothing to do with nerves.

Just then, Miss Newlands came rushing up.

"Quick, Damien. Mrs Alcock's just realised. You have to wear Manjit's T-shirt."

"What?" I said, bemused. Then I realised Mannie's character has this awful, grubby T-shirt. Mine was fresh from the laundry pile.

"Quick!" said Miss Newlands. "It's nearly time for you to go into the wings."

"But..." I was very aware of Jessica and the Giggling Gits.

"Just do it!" snapped Miss Newlands. "We've all seen a boy's chest before!"

As fast as I could, I ripped off my T-shirt.

Gales of giggles. Loads of Looks.

"Ooh, Damien's got a six-pack!"

More insane laughter.

I hitched up my jeans with as much dignity as I could muster. "Just shut up!" I snapped. Thank goodness we were called into the wings just then. I could hide my bright-red cheeks in the dark.

But the Giggling Gits hadn't finished with me yet. Being cramped up in the dark in a small space with (shock, horror!) a BOY was too much for them.

"Did you have a nice time with Jessica?" said one.

"Is she your girlfriend?" giggled another.

I glanced round for Jessica, but I couldn't see her. She made her entrance further upstage, so was in a different part of the wings. I just hoped she hadn't heard the Gits. They had been so loud.

"You do realise the audience might hear you?" I muttered, as coolly as I could. "You're supposed to be silent in the wings."

"Good job Nick isn't here then," said the chief Git. "He can never do what he's supposed to do."

"Yeah, where is he, Damien?" said another. "Shouldn't he be here?"

I felt as if a bucket of cold water had been chucked down my back. With all the excitement of rehearsing with Jessica, I'd completely forgotten about him. I peered along the wing. There was safety lighting but it was still very dark. Nick is tall and skinny. I was sure he wasn't there and I couldn't see Mrs Laing, either. Maybe she had thought that once Nick was in the wing, he would stay there. *Bonkers*.

It was like plunging into a nightmare. I guessed we had about five minutes before we were on – but that gave Nick time to find that ladder again. Any moment now, he could be on the 'trampoline', ruining the performance and getting himself into really serious trouble. I had no choice.

"Excuse me," I whispered to the people next to me and slipped past them, making for the backstage door. To my horror, I could see Miss Newlands between me and my goal. There was no way I would get past without her noticing.

"I've got to go to the loo!" I hissed, urgently.

"Well, for goodness' sake be quick!" she said.

There wasn't much more light backstage than there had been in the wings.

"Damien!" It was a loud whisper. I nearly jumped out of my skin and whipped round with a yelp.

"Sorry," said the voice. "It's me, Jessica. Where are you going? The loos are the other way."

I had to think quickly. Could I trust her? Or would she let me down and start clucking like her mother? I didn't think so.

"Nick's gone," I said. "I daren't tell Miss. It's the third time this evening. She'll go ballistic."

"What is it with Nick?" said Jessica, looking puzzled. "I mean, he's obviously not stupid..."

"Stupid? *Stupid*? He's a genius! But no one seems to understand that. It drives me mad."

"I'll help you look," said Jessica.

My jaw dropped. Was this Miss Sweet and Innocent, the Worksheet Wonder?

"Don't just stand there," she said. "Where shall we try first?"

"He found this ladder," I said quickly. "He said it led to this huge mesh trampoline thing above the stage."

"I know what it is," said Jessica. "They hang the lights from it. Didn't you notice it when we had the dress rehearsal?"

I shook my head. "I don't even know where the ladder is. But I bet that's where he's gone."

"We'd better split up," said Jessica. "It'll be quicker. You go that way and I'll go this."

I really, really didn't want her to go, but I knew she was right. The theatre wasn't huge but we had very little time.

"OK," I said. "If you find him and he argues, tell him Damien'll bash him if he doesn't come straight away."

Then I ran like the wind.

I was lucky. I didn't meet anyone. All the kids were in drama studios or dressing rooms, waiting for their calls. No teachers were prowling about backstage. I did hear somebody yell, "Hey, you!" but I ignored it. I was beginning to get the hang of the layout of the theatre now. It didn't take long to check that there was no ladder the way

I had gone. I ran back and nearly crashed into Jessica, who had discovered the same on the other side.

"No luck?" she said.

I shook my head. "We'll have to go back!" I said. "It must be time for us to go on!"

Jessica grabbed my arm. "The lighting box!" she said. "Maybe the ladder is up there!"

Why hadn't I thought of that? It was on the side that I'd checked. We hared back along the corridor and through the door marked 'Technicians Only'. We tiptoed up the stairs. At the top, there was a door with a small window. Through it, we could see two technicians working at the sound and lighting boards. But beside it, flat against the wall, was a ladder.

"I'll keep watch," said Jessica. I nodded and started to climb, praying that this was where Nick had gone. I can't describe how relieved I felt when I got to the top and saw a dark, skinny shape, hunched at the edge of the 'trampoline'.

"Nick!" I hissed. "Come here! Quick!"

Nick turned at my voice. I beckoned madly. I could sense his reluctance, but he started to come towards me.

"What?" he said.

From where I was, I could see through the mesh right down into the auditorium. One or two faces lifted. They had heard Nick speak. I put my finger on my lips and beckoned again. Seconds later, Nick was at the top of the ladder and I started to go down.

"Damien, it's just amazing up here!" he said, in awestruck tones.

I sighed. He would have no idea why he was in trouble again.

Below me I heard voices.

"I was looking for the toilet," Jessica was saying. "But I got lost."

I froze, willing the technician or teacher or whoever it was, not to look up.

"Why have you stopped?" asked Nick.

I grabbed his ankle and squeezed it hard, hoping he would get the message. Fortunately, the man below us was busy explaining to Jessica where the toilets were. Then I heard the door of the lighting box shut.

Moments later, we were in the backstage corridor, where Jessica was waiting for us.

"Run!" I shouted at Nick and we all hurtled back as fast as we could.

Would we be in time?

We rounded the corner, and the sight I was dreading met my eyes.

Queen Hen, bright red in the face, was in full squawk. Miss Newlands and Mr Burn were standing up to it but poor Mrs Laing looked pecked to death. Over-excited kids had escaped from the wing and had gathered around, twittering.

"Jessica! Nick! Damien!" Mrs Laing croaked when she saw us and promptly burst into tears, but it was the Queen Hen herself who provided the real shock.

"Quick! She's falling!" I said and rushed forwards to stop her. I flung my arms as far as I could round her waist and braced my legs. "Help me!" I gasped. "She weighs a tonne!"

Fortunately for me, Mr Burn and Jessica were more alert than everyone else.

"It's OK, we've got her," said Jessica and as gently as we could, with plenty of help now that everyone else had woken up, we lowered her to the ground.

"Is she dead?" asked one of the Giggling Gits.

"Don't be so stupid!" I growled. I had really had enough.

Mr Burn was heaving the Queen Hen onto her

side. "Stand back, everyone," he said. "I'm a First Aider. She's fainted."

"Recovery position," said Nick, sounding interested. As ever, he was completely unaware of the trouble he had caused.

"Oh shut up," I said, suddenly feeling very tired.

Just then, applause burst from the auditorium.

"Oh my goodness!" said Miss Newlands. "We're on!"

We all bundled back into the wings, falling over each other in the rush to get to our places. My head was in a whirl. I had never felt less like stepping out onto a stage.

"Go on!" hissed Miss Newlands, giving me a little shove. "You've caused enough hassle tonight. Get out there and do your stuff!"

Honestly! Teachers! She must have been taking lessons in encouragement from the Queen Hen!

I staggered onto the stage and huddled into a little ball, cringing. That was OK. That was what I felt like doing – but it was also what I was meant to do. When I heard Jessica telling me I was a complete loser, in just the same nasty, spiteful voice she'd used when we were rehearsing, I knew it would be all right. We could do it.

Afterwards, when it was all over, Nick, Jessica and I were called for an audience before the Queen Hen's throne. She had been found a comfortable seat in the foyer and, I suspect, a stiff drink.

She cleared her throat. "Thank you, Damien," she croaked, and I thought she might faint again with the effort. "I believe I have you to thank for saving me from a nasty fall."

"S'all right, Miss."

"But what on earth you all thought you were doing, wandering off like that just before you were due to go on, I have absolutely no idea.

"As for you, Jessica, I am utterly shocked. I would never have thought that a sensible girl like you would get yourself involved with such silly, silly boys as these."

"But, Miss..." said Jessica, looking startled.

"That will do," said the Queen Hen. "In the end, you performed creditably enough and did not show us all up in front of our famous visitor! Now let's see if we can have no further trouble before we go home, please! Off you go."

Jessica still looked astonished.

I shook my head. "*Bonkers*," I said. "She's a hopeless case."

"I always thought that it was you, Nick and Mannie," said Jessica. "I thought you really were silly... well, maybe not you but..."

"Nope," I said. "Innocent victims, us."

"And me," she said thoughtfully. "Now."

"Yep. Join the club."

She gave me a conspiratorial smile and a very small, very sensible giggle. Not The Look. Absolutely not The Look. "OK," she said. "Sounds like fun."

I sighed. *I am bonkers*, I thought. *A hopeless case. I am totally bonkers about Jessica Laing.*

THE RESIDENTIAL
BY FRANCIS MCCRICKARD

Eyes like a fierce animal, that's what Beenisha saw. Eyes glinting in the dark of the forest; eyes wide and roaring with thoughts of killing and satisfying hunger.

"Beenisha, come and look at this book."

Beenisha reached forward towards the eyes and touched...

the pale green wall and two dents in the plaster that the back of a carelessly pushed chair had made in the classroom wall.

She slumped to the floor in a faint.

As Miss Sanderson saw to Beenisha, and her classmates chattered all around her, Molly Baines finished the sentence she was writing, placed a full stop very firmly at the end, and put her pencil down exactly two centimetres (she measured the gap) to the right of her English workbook and in line with the edge. The workbook was slightly askew, so she straightened it and then adjusted the position of the pencil. The bottom of the right sleeve of her blue school jumper had been turned down when it brushed against the edge of the table. She carefully turned it back up.

Trevor Barre, the head teacher, came into the classroom. When he saw what had happened, he ushered Miss Sanderson back, away from the rest of the children. "It's going to take time with Beenisha," he said. "I know it's not going to be easy..."

"She's hardly said a word since she got here."

Both teachers looked across the classroom. Beenisha had forced herself into the corner, where the ends of two bookshelves didn't quite meet, and was squatting there with her head in her hands.

"...and this fainting..."

"Given what happened back in her own country, it's not surprising. She's seen things no child should ever see."

Molly Baines opened her reading book, taking care, as always, not to crack the spine. She placed the edge of a sheet of paper under each line before reading it. As she moved the paper steadily down the page, Molly noticed that the clear varnish on her nails was chipped badly. She would redo them at home that evening.

"Beenisha needs a lot more than we can give her."

"She's going to get individual help soon. That's what I came to tell you. It'll be in place after she comes back from the residential."

"She can't come to Castlemount, Trevor! I mean, for one thing, who's she going to share a room with?"

The head teacher swayed from one foot to the other. He beamed to the class and rocked from side to side. "The residential could be just the thing! Bring her out of herself!" Then he spun quickly and left the room.

Before Miss Sanderson could stop them, all the class, except Beenisha and Molly, who was studying her nails, rose to their feet and swayed from side to side, lifting one foot and then the other.

"It's in the Dales."

"What are *Dales*?"

"Wide valleys, with beautiful rivers flowing through them. But we call the whole area the *Yorkshire Dales*. There are hills as well. Some of you must have been to them. They'll be very green now that spring is here."

Four children had been to Torremolinos; two to Mallorca; two went regularly to the Primrose Caravan Park at Filey; one to a chalet in Brid; three had been to Orlando; two to Pakistan. Reef's Dad was a semi-professional surfer and they always went to Cornwall for their holidays. Rosie Paynter thought she'd been to Hong Kong where the chips were nice but there wasn't enough ketchup. Darren and Joanne had been to Ilkley, which Miss Sanderson thought was just in the Dales, otherwise no one in the class had explored the beautiful, extensive countryside that started barely 20 miles from their city. Others had travelled great distances but not to go on holidays: Ali and Nasir had come from Somalia; Jonas from Zimbabwe; the twins, Raneen and Zainab from Iraq, and Beenisha was from the Congo.

"Let's hope all this rain stops! Don't forget strong shoes for the walks!" They were excited in spite of the rain. Only one day to go.

There were two beds in each room. Everyone chose who they would share with, but Miss Sanderson *told* Molly Baines that she would be with Beenisha.

"But, Miss, she never says anything and she's not really my friend."

"I know that, Molly, but you are a very sensible girl. I can trust you. Beenisha needs a good friend. You know she's had a terrible time; her parents, brothers, all killed. Try to understand what she's been through..."

This was hard for Molly. The class had done special project work on Kenya in Year 5 and learned about its different tribes, their costumes, dances, the ways they farmed, and the wildlife parks. Molly knew that some African countries, including Beenisha's, had a lot of problems with wars and famines, but that still left her a long way from being able to imagine what Beenisha had been through.

Anyway, Molly didn't want to imagine anything like that! Once, lying in bed on a warm summer night when she couldn't get to sleep, she had wondered what it would be like if she lost her parents. She imagined coming home after school one day, finding no one there and waiting until a police car pulled up outside. "Now then, young Molly, I have to tell you that there's been a terrible accident..." Molly had shivered even though she was hot. The only *real* fright she had ever had was when she was eight, and her dad had hospital tests done to a lump on his neck. Her mum told her that he might have to have a serious operation. Molly cried herself to sleep that night. The lump was benign, the operation was simple and he didn't die, but that was bad enough, thought Molly.

Molly couldn't understand what Beenisha had been through. She had tried to make friends when the African girl had first joined their class, but Beenisha hadn't responded. She could speak some English but most of the time chose not to say anything. Sometimes she growled like an animal. There was no doubt about it, Beenisha was weird and it wasn't fair that Molly had to share a room with her.

Beenisha sat in the window seat alongside Miss Sanderson for the journey to Castlemount. She stared at cityscape and the countryside but didn't see them.

Molly sat on her own at the front of the coach to see exactly where they were going. The other children kept asking questions.

"Is there a castle there?"

"No. It gets its name because there are some rocks that look a bit like a castle. But it is an old building and there's a big wood that almost surrounds it."

"Is there somewhere to play football?"

"Are there any shops?"

"Is there a place to buy sweets?"

"Can we stay up till midnight?"

"Are there ghosts?"

"Can I phone me mum when we get there?"

"Do they have ketchup?"

"Are we nearly there yet?"

Darren thought it was a great joke to keep repeating that last question, until Miss Sanderson told him that it wasn't too late to turn around and go back to Leeds.

They travelled for two hours, a long way into the Dales. The last 30 minutes was on narrow, twisting lanes, where every car they met had to reverse and pull into the entrance to a field so that the coach could pass. The rain had stopped. It was a beautiful, clear spring day.

Molly wasn't sure she wanted to get to the Centre. Once they reached Castlemount, they would be given their rooms; she would have to spend some time alone with Beenisha and she wasn't looking forward to that.

As they turned off the road and on to a gravel track that rose up the side of a steep hill, Miss Sanderson pointed out the Centre buildings, the dense wood that almost completely surrounded them and the sheer, rugged crags below and to the left.

"You're going to climb down those rocks on ropes," she told the children. It's called abseiling."

"No way," said Molly to herself and fixed her gaze on a stream, swollen by days and days of heavy rain, that exploded over the top of the rocks and tumbled down a cleft. She shivered. "I hope the rooms are warm."

Norman, a large, smiling man dressed in an old, saggy grey jumper and combat trousers with pockets everywhere, greeted them as they got off the coach.

"I'll show you round and tell you a few dos and don'ts; mainly dos, I'm pleased to say."

They all followed Norman into the main building. Molly didn't want to get her new trainers dirty and stepped carefully around the puddles in the car park.

Beenisha went missing after the evening meal on the first evening.

"She can't have gone far," said Philip Thompson, a classroom assistant, who had come along to help Miss Sanderson. "Probably a bit disorientated."

"That's putting it mildly, Phil."

Beenisha stood as still as the stones that gave Castlemount its name. She was completely hidden behind one of the long curtains in the main meeting room. The big picture window faced west on the only side of the building that wasn't sheltered by the extensive woodland; it gave a long view of the valley with its jigsaw of fields and its twisting river. The sun, huge and deep red, was setting gently and had mesmerised Beenisha. She had watched many sunsets in her native country, the sudden drop into the flat land and the quick darkness, but this reminded her of one specifically, and a night she could never forget.

"We will stop here, children," Beenisha's mother had said.

After the soldiers took her father, Beenisha and the rest of the family had run for over an hour, deep into the forest, and they were exhausted.

"It will be dark soon and there is no path. I can hear water nearby. This is a good place." *Beenisha's mother pulled Beenisha and her two small brothers close, hugged them and told them not to be afraid.*

"Look at the sun before it leaves the sky. Tomorrow, it will come again. The day after, it will come again. Now there seems to be no light in our lives, but there will be. There is always goodness and it always finds you again. Never forget that. *Beenisha's mother set a fire with dry grass and twigs and sent Beenisha to collect firewood. "We will eat and I will tell you stories and then we will sleep a long and deep sleep."*

The sun along the English valley had almost disappeared. Beenisha shook the stillness out of her head and as she did, quick movements in the wood to the right of the buildings caught her eye.

The wood was now so dark, she could barely make out shapes, but there *was* something. She saw something move in the gloom, some*one* perhaps. Yes, it *was* someone, and Beenisha saw a shape like an arm. It *was* an arm. She watched it rise slowly and come down swiftly, rise and fall, rise and fall. Something metal in the hand, a blade, caught the last of the light and glinted.

Beenisha watched the hand and the blade rise and fall, rise and fall, rise and fall on her mother and her brothers and, as it did, she ran further into the forest and hid, hid for days, wide-eyed with wild animals prowling about her while her mother and brothers and father slept the long, deep sleep.

Beenisha slumped to the floor of the meeting room in a faint.

"It's not fair."

"I know it's not easy, Molly, but try to be a good friend to Beenisha. I'll be right next door, so there's no need to worry."

Molly undressed and put on her pyjamas in the small *en-suite* bathroom. They were thick, pale-blue flannelette with yellow ducks all over them. She took longer than usual in the bathroom.

She wiped her toothbrush very carefully and put it and her toothpaste and soap neatly alongside each other on the narrow glass shelf over the sink, adjusting their positions several times. Then she took her time rubbing moisturiser into the skin of her face and hands like her mother said she should always do last thing at night.

Beenisha was already in bed and looked as if she was asleep when Molly came out of the bathroom. Sharing a room with her might be easier than she had thought but Molly still felt sad. In the other rooms, her classmates would all be chatting excitedly, frightening each other with ghost stories, planning midnight feasts, spreading tales of Reef, who said he was going to kiss Lucy sometime on the residential.

Molly said goodnight, but Beenisha didn't reply.

The wind woke Molly up. She looked at the travel clock her mum had packed for her. It was half-past two in the morning. She had never been awake at that time before. The room was cold. Beenisha was dressed and stood at the window. She had drawn the curtains wide. The calm of the day had vanished. The wind was fierce. Clouds scuttled like huge rats across the hills on the other side of the valley, half-obscuring a huge moon. Beenisha stared at the wood.

"Listen," said Beenisha, without turning.

Molly listened. The wind was in the roof of the building. The sound was like ripples, waves – no, Beenisha knew what it was the sound of – it was soldiers marching, chanting, coming closer. When Molly crossed the room to the window, she saw that Beenisha was shaking and sweating. She put her arm around her shoulder. It was awkward because Beenisha was taller than Molly.

"It's all right, Beenisha. It's all right." For the first time she noticed three scars; short, slanting lines high on Beenisha's cheeks.

"My parents are in the woods!"

She said *parents* so that it sounded like *parrents*. She is weird, thought Molly. Her parents are dead. Miss Sanderson said so. That's why she came to Leeds. She hugged Beenisha harder.

"The soldiers are coming for them!"

"There are no soldiers, Beenisha, and you're parents are... your parents are not here."

Beenisha pushed Molly's arm off her shoulder and went to the door of the room.

"They will kill them. They will kill my parents and my brothers."

"But they're d... they're not here, Beenisha!"

Beenisha ran out of the room and into the long corridor. Hardly stopping to think except to force her feet into her trainers, Molly went after her. Beenisha went left towards the emergency exit, the one they had been told they must use *only in an emergency*. With one push on the bar, it opened, a security light came on, and Beenisha stepped outside into its glare. Molly passed Miss Sanderson's room, heard her teacher snoring and, without thinking, followed Beenisha through the emergency door before it swung shut automatically. This was stupid! Beenisha was halfway down the stairs. Molly called, but softly. Her voice was smothered by the wind. Beenisha didn't turn but scampered quickly down the rest of the steps and ran towards the dark wood.

When Molly reached the bottom of the steps, she hesitated. This was wrong! She should go back; get Miss Sanderson. This was dangerous! The wood terrified her. Its dark outline was like a huge, wild animal, crouched, waiting to pounce. The trees close together, bending in the wind, were already reaching out to try to grab her. Molly wasn't going to go into the wood. She had never been in a wood alone, not even in the few trees they called a wood in the little park next to her estate in Leeds. Woods were frightening. Molly didn't understand them. She understood pavements and bricks and concrete, lawns and little hedges, houses and shops.

Beenisha raced through a forest that was thousands of miles away from Castlemount but this time she was not running away to hide. No, this time she was running to stop the soldiers, to save her mother and brothers.

Molly ran as fast as she could back to the emergency door but couldn't open it from the outside. She banged on the door. Miss Sanderson would hear her in spite of the wind. At that moment, the wind took a deep breath and there was silence apart from a soft rustling in the tops of the trees. Molly thought she heard her name being called and then the wind blew again more fiercely than ever. Beenisha was calling her. She remembered Miss Sanderson's words: "Be a good friend to Beenisha. Look after her." Molly banged on the door, banged again and again until she hurt her hands. No one came. What Molly did next was stupid, she knew, and she'd never done anything remotely like it before. She was a careful girl but, that night, she couldn't help herself.

She would go and find Beenisha and bring her back. Beenisha would be just inside the wood. It would only take a few minutes and nothing would happen to her. She raced back down the stairs, across the grass and into the dark trees.

Beenisha wasn't just inside the wood.

She won't be far, thought Molly and kept thinking that as she ran deeper and deeper into the wood, sure that with every step she would find Beenisha. Each branch that touched her was a claw of the creature that had been waiting for her, a claw that tried to grab and pull her into the undergrowth. Each faint sound, a rustle, a crack, was a frightening roar from that creature.

Molly wanted the wind to blow harder, make thunder in the treetops and drown these small, terrifying sounds. Don't stop running, she told herself, and then they can't, can't, can't grab you.

Her lungs ached she was going so fast and breathing so hard. She told her imagination to calm down. She tried to remember what she had seen in daylight. Year 6 had been allowed quarter of an hour to explore outside but only close to the building, not the wood. "We'll go there together tomorrow," Miss Sanderson had said. "The bluebells are just out. Beautiful!"

Now, for Molly, the beautiful bluebells were part of the black, threatening mass all around her. Stumbling at every other step but managing to keep upright, she ran as fast as she could, tripping over fallen branches and tendrils of bramble that tugged at her pyjama bottoms and scratched her ankles.

The moon's light found a gap in the clouds and in the trees just ahead. Molly came to a wide path. The creature couldn't grab her if she stayed in the middle of the path. Feeling safer, Molly stopped and listened. Beenisha stepped from the dark bushes on Molly's right. Molly jumped.

"You came," Beenisha said.

"You called me."

Beenisha shook her head. "I didn't. Come this way. There is water. You can hear it. My mother will be there, and my brothers." She took Molly's hand and ran along the path calling for her mother, "Maamu! Maamu!"

Molly tried to slow her down – they should go back to the Centre – but Beenisha was too strong and had a firm grip on her wrist. The moon disappeared behind the clouds again and they ran on in near-darkness. The path narrowed and turned sharply, but in the dark and because they were running so fast, they didn't see this and fell headlong down the steep bank of the stream.

Frantically, they tried to grab a tree root, a tussock of grass, a bush, anything to stop themselves but they were tumbling downwards so wildly that it was impossible. Below, the water snarled animal-like as it rushed through a narrow rock channel towards Castlemount crags, where it crashed 30 metres down the rock face.

If they couldn't control their fall, the angry stream would take Beenisha and Molly there. It seemed that the wood itself was pushing them closer to the hungry, growling torrent. Both of them felt weak and had almost given up trying to save themselves from falling into the water when, suddenly, the wood relented. Halfway down the bank the earth curved outwards, forming a broad shelf. Their momentum slowed here and they were able to grab branches that were lying firmly fixed to the earth. They came to a halt.

Molly told herself she shouldn't have left the room, shouldn't have left her bed, shouldn't have come on the trip. She held back the tears. "Are you all right, Beenisha?"

"I think so, Molly."

"You used my name." It was the first time

Beenisha had used Molly's name, anyone's name, as far as Molly knew.

"You are my friend," replied Beenisha.

Molly felt pain and put her hand to her forehead. It was bleeding.

"You are hurt, Molly," said Beenisha.

Suddenly, before Molly had a chance to reply, the earth they were lying on moved, a gentle ripple to start with and then an eruption that threw them backwards.

Molly screamed as she fell and screamed again as she saw a huge, dark form emerge from the bank like a great, fat worm. The worm grew longer and then stood upright, towering over them.

Beenisha groped about in the dark, found a stick and jumped up, brandishing it. "I will kill you!" she yelled.

"Nice of you to drop in," the huge man answered. "There's no need to kill me."

Sobbing, Molly scrambled back up the bank away from the stranger. Beenisha swung the stick wildly. "Get away! Get away!"

"Whoa! Slow down, young lady! It's me, Norman. Don't you recognise me? I'm in charge of Castlemount. Let me get a lamp."

Norman pulled a lamp from his hide, a small depression dug into the bank and roofed by a latticework of branches covered with clods of earth and stones. Once he had lit it and the girls calmed down, he rang Miss Sanderson on her mobile and told her that Molly and Beenisha were with him and safe. He let both girls speak to their teacher. Next, Norman got a flask of hot tea and a first-aid kit from the hide. He cleaned and dressed Molly's wound, which was stinging fiercely.

"It'll hurt but it's not much more than a graze. You'll be fine."

"I've got my pyjamas dirty."

"They'll wash."

He gave Beenisha a blanket and Molly his jacket to wrap around themselves. As he poured the tea and they shared the cup, Norman told them about his hobby.

"Wildlife photography: my photos are all over the walls at Castlemount. Tonight, I've been watching badgers. There's a sett just over on the other bank. The noise you made's sent them underground. You're not likely to see them now."

"Sorry," said Molly.

Norman laughed. "There's no need to apologise, young lady, but you do need to tell me what you're doing out here in the middle of this wild night, rolling down river banks. And, as soon as you've had your tea, I'll get you back to your beds. Miss Sanderson said they've been worried sick back at the Centre. You must never, never do anything like this again."

Norman deliberately took them a long way back to Castlemount, on paths through the wood that only he knew. He wanted them to see that it was not a frightening place; he wanted to clear the ghosts out of both their heads.

As they walked, the clouds scattered and the big moon ruled the night sky, shining brightly through the branches. They worked out that when Beenisha had watched the sunset, she had seen Norman cutting branches for a new hide he was making.

"That was just silly old me," he said. "Wouldn't harm a fly."

On their way, they sighted serious owls and a curious fox, but no soldiers.

"I reckon you've chased them right out of these parts and they're never coming back again. You stood right up to them, my girl. You didn't run away and hide."

As they approached the Centre, it looked as if every single light was on. Norman patted Beenisha gently on the shoulder. "I hope you've chased them out of your head as well," he said, "but maybe that'll take a bit longer."

"I think it is going to happen, Mr Norman," replied Beenisha, "because now I have a special friend in England who was very brave for me. I was not alone in the forest. My mother told me goodness always finds you again. Molly is goodness."

Molly smiled broadly. "Not just one friend," she said. "Look!"

Shortly after Beenisha and Molly left the building, Miss Sanderson had been woken by a knocking on her door. Lucy had come to tell her that Joanne had a stomachache, was crying and wanted to go home. When Miss Sanderson saw the door to the room next to hers was wide open and the girls missing, she and Mr Thompson had searched every room and cupboard in Castlemount, and woken and questioned every child before telephoning the police. Now all the members of Year 6 stood at their bedroom windows looking down at the two police cars that had just arrived. When Beenisha and Molly stepped into the brilliance of the security lights and looked up, they all waved and shouted wildly.

"You have lots of friends," said Molly.

The week went by too quickly for Molly and Beenisha. They were never out of each other's company for long and always worked together on the activities. Whenever Beenisha didn't understand something that Norman or one of the other leaders was explaining, Molly helped her. Whenever Molly didn't think she could do one of the activities, especially the abseiling, Beenisha encouraged her and gave her confidence. When the class had to decipher clues and follow a trail that had been set in the wood, it was Molly and Beenisha who finished first.

"We could have done it in the dark," Molly told Mrs Sanderson.

"Don't even think about it!" replied their teacher, but then smiled and put her arms round both of them.

On Friday, pupils, teachers and parents were outside school waiting to greet the coach when it returned. As soon as she stepped down, Miss Sanderson spoke to the head teacher.

"Trevor, you know you said you were getting special help for Beenisha," she smiled. "Well, I think she's already got it."

tHE LIE
BY SOPHIE MCKENZIE

Spencer stopped. There was the school. Hundreds of blue-uniformed kids streaming through a high, steel gate at the end of the road.

Spencer hesitated, then checked his own uniform. It looked OK, he thought. Not too neat; not too scruffy. It was second-hand, of course. All his clothes were second-hand. He sighed. At least Dad had bought the right uniform this time. At Spencer's last school – and there'd been two others in the past five years since Mum died – Dad had splashed out on three white T-shirts. Great, except they were supposed to be polo shirts.

It wasn't a big deal. But it hadn't helped.

"Hi. You're Spencer Sykes, aren't you?"

Spencer turned round. A chubby girl with short, spiky red hair stood in front of him. Unlike most of the girls, she wore blue trousers instead of a skirt.

"Yeah," he said. "How d'you know?"

"They said you were starting in our class last week." The girl smiled. "Also, I saw you moving in at the weekend. I live in your block. I'm Amy, by the way. Your dad has a really cool bike."

"Oh." Spencer didn't know what to say.

"Come on," Amy said. "I'll show you where everything is." She took his arm and led him through the gates.

Spencer thought this was a bit bossy, but mostly he felt relieved to meet someone friendly.

The school was a large, brick building – smaller and smarter than either of Spencer's last schools. Anxiety tugged at his stomach. Dad had said Rayburn Park was just an ordinary primary school. But Dad got stuff wrong all the time. Suppose the kids who went here were really smart? Or really rich? Or really cool?

Amy led Spencer across the playground and through an open door. Most of the kids milling about were shorter than Spencer, which made him feel a bit better. They walked along a maze of corridors. That didn't faze him – he'd been through all this before. After two days, he knew from experience, this building would be as familiar to him as his own home.

"Changing rooms are down there." Amy pointed through a set of double doors. "Toilets next door."

"Thanks."

"This is our room." Amy opened another door.

Spencer stared at the rows of tables and chairs. It was a lot nicer than his last classroom, with a big square window by the teacher's desk and lots of brightly coloured artwork on the walls. All the same, the knot of anxiety in his stomach tightened. He'd never fit in here.

"Oi, Amy, you fatso, who's your boyfriend?"

Spencer spun round.

The boy who had spoken was tall – the same height as Spencer – but, unlike Spencer, his white shirt hung loose over his navy trousers and his pale-blue tie was tied into the tiniest of knots about halfway down his chest.

"Shut up, Kieran," Amy said. "He's not my boyfriend. This is Spencer."

"Well, hi there, Spencer."

"Hi." Spencer smiled, but instead of smiling back, Kieran crossed his arms and leant against the wall.

Spencer's heart beat faster. He'd been here before. He knew Kieran was weighing him up;

deciding whether to accept him or not. Spencer looked round. The other kids were watching Kieran to see what he did next – like, however he treated Spencer, they would do the same.

The next few minutes were crucial. Spencer panicked. He pointed to the MP3 player sticking out of Kieran's shirt pocket.

"Nice PortoDec," he said.

Kieran looked down at the machine. "'S'alright. I'm getting the new version for Christmas – you know, the NanoDec that's just come out?"

"Christmas is two months away," Spencer said.

Damn. That sounded stupid.

"Du-uh!" Kieran rolled his eyes. The two boys nearest him laughed. Spencer's heart beat even faster. He was making himself look like an idiot.

"I didn't mean Christmas was two months away," he said quickly. "I meant, I know how you could get a NanoDec sooner."

Oh no. Why had he said that? Out of the corner of his eye, Spencer could see Amy watching him curiously.

"Yeah?" Kieran frowned. "How?"

"He's talking crap," said the boy next to Kieran.

"I'm not. Er... it's my dad. He's... he's a music producer," Spencer lied.

"Really?" Kieran's eyes narrowed. "What's that got to do with getting me a NanoDec?"

Spencer glanced round. Half the class was watching. Whatever he did next would decide how he would fit into this class.

For ever.

"Just that my dad loves all that technical stuff. Especially when new things come out. He's always got loads of gadgets lying about at home."

This last bit was true at least – Dad's latest job was as a motorbike courier for an electronic products company, so he did – often – have gadgets in the house ready for the next day's early-morning delivery.

"Gadgets... you mean like NanoDecs?" Kieran said.

"Yeah, loads of them."

"So you could get one off him for me?"

"Course. No problem." The words were out of Spencer's mouth before he could stop them.

"Tomorrow?"

"Er... I dunno." Spencer's head was spinning. How had this happened? Why had he even mentioned freaking NanoDecs? They were the latest, coolest MP3 players on the market. So new, you couldn't even buy one second-hand.

"Can I have one, too?" This was the boy standing next to Kieran.

"Yeah, and me." This came from a girl standing near Amy, who was still watching Spencer curiously, her head to one side.

"Look, I can probably get my dad to give me *one*," Spencer blustered. "But no way more than that."

"Right, well I asked first," Kieran said.

"OK," Spencer said. "But I don't know about tomorrow."

"He's making it up," said the girl next to Amy.

"I'm not," Spencer insisted. "It's just I don't know if my dad will have any NanoDecs in the house."

"But a minute ago, you said he had loads of them," Kieran said.

"Yeah, he does, it's just..." Spencer looked round. He knew that if he said he couldn't deliver a NanoDec now, he was sunk. He took a deep breath. "No problem. I'll bring one in tomorrow."

"Great." Kieran grinned, gesturing towards a table at the back of the room. "Come and sit with me."

Spencer followed him to the table, feeling numb. How on earth was he was going to get his hands on a NanoDec by tomorrow morning?

It was a long day. Spencer sat with Kieran in class and at lunch. When it came to break, Kieran organised a football game and let Spencer play on his team. Amy tried to speak to Spencer a couple of times, but Kieran told her to go away. Which she did. She didn't seem to have many friends, Spencer noticed, though most people weren't as rude to her as Kieran was.

When the bell rang for the end of school, Kieran was first out the door. Spencer followed as quickly as he could. He wanted to get away before Amy had a chance to walk home with him. He also wanted some time to think.

Dad was in the flat when he got there, slumped in front of the TV, as usual. He was still in his motorbike leathers. When Mum was alive, he used to change when he got home from work. Not now.

"Hi," he looked up. "How was school?"

"Fine." Spencer shrugged. "No problem. Er... I need some money to buy some stuff, though."

"Sorry, son." Dad yawned. "No can do. Maybe in

a few weeks. Now we're living nearer the shop, they might give me a few more deliveries."

Spencer sighed. He went into the kitchen and made himself a sandwich and Dad a cup of tea. They sat and watched a couple of *Top Gear* repeats together, then Dad found a programme on motorbikes and cracked open a beer.

Spencer was flicking through a magazine, not concentrating on the pictures, just worrying, when Dad called out.

"I've left tomorrow's delivery on the Bonnie. Bring it inside will you, son?"

"Sure." Normally Spencer hated it when Dad asked him to do stuff like that – which he did a lot. Dad was always forgetting things. But right now he was glad of the distraction. He jogged downstairs to Dad's Triumph 650 Bonneville, which was parked in the front yard of the apartment block.

Spencer wasn't massively into bikes, but he knew quite a lot about them – hard not to, they were Dad's big obsession. Spencer unlocked the pannier. He peered inside.

No way.

An open, half-full box of NanoDecs was lying on top. Spencer laughed out loud. It was too easy, like fate was saying: *here*, *present for you*, *Spencer*. Like he was *meant* to take one.

Except, of course, that he couldn't. These weren't Spencer's MP3 players. They weren't even Dad's. Just stuff he had to deliver the next morning. Couriers didn't normally keep deliveries in their homes overnight, but Electrical Showstoppers was a small, local business that allowed the couriers to make their own arrangements. And Dad liked getting up as late as possible.

All this went through Spencer's mind in a few seconds. He glanced again at the box of NanoDecs. The delivery note lay on top; the company name Electrical Showstoppers written in large type on it.

There had to be at least 20 NanoDecs here. Surely no one would notice if *one* went missing. Spencer took one out of the box. The slim, silver oblong with its oval screen was clearly visible inside the bright-blue packaging. He folded his jumper over it and tucked the jumper under his arm.

"Hi, Spencer," said a girl's voice. "Thought I saw you out here."

Spencer started. Amy was standing beside him,

staring at Dad's bike. Her eyes rested on the open pannier. The delivery note was still on top of the box. Spencer slammed the pannier lid shut. Had Amy seen him take the NanoDec and hide it in his jumper?

"What are you doing here?" he said.

"I live here, remember?" Amy grinned. "Your dad's bike is *so* cool, isn't it?"

"I suppose." Spencer could feel himself reddening. "He's into all that retro stuff."

"It's a really nice bike." Amy laid a pudgy arm on the handlebars. "My brother's got a 650 twin, too – a Kawasaki, you know?"

"Yeah." Spencer forced a smile. The Kawasaki Z650 twin engine was one of the few non-British bikes Dad had time for. "I know."

"Mum hates it, but I think it's really cool," Amy said. "Sometimes my brother takes me on the back of it. Does your dad do that?"

Spencer hugged the folded jumper more tightly under his arm. "I guess." He felt even more awkward now.

Amy stared at him. She looked a little put out. Spencer's cheeks burned more fiercely.

"OK." Amy hesitated. "Well, see you later."

"Bye." Spencer waited until she'd got inside,

then took the box of NanoDecs out of the pannier, re-locked it and trudged inside. He handed the box to Dad, then took his jumper and the stolen package into his room.

He sat on the narrow bed and thought... If Dad didn't notice anything was missing, then he would keep the NanoDec and hand it over to Kieran. If he did notice, Spencer could pretend to look for it, make out it had somehow fallen out of the box and hand it back.

Spencer put the NanoDec under his bed and went back to Dad, who was opening another beer. He sat on the sofa and waited. But Dad didn't open up the box or check the NanoDecs against the delivery note. In fact, the only time he got up from his chair all evening, was to put some oven chips on for tea.

Dad had gone off on his delivery route by the time Spencer woke the next morning. He checked for the NanoDec straight away. Still there, under his jumper. Well, if Dad hadn't noticed any cartons missing from the box, maybe no one would...

Two hours later, everything Spencer had hoped for appeared to have come true. Kieran was clearly impressed by the NanoDec, though he did his best not to show it. The whole class was treating Spencer with total respect.

When the bell rang for morning break, Amy came over. "Where d'you get that NanoDec for Kieran?" she said.

"My dad's a music producer. He's got loads of stuff like that just lying around." Spencer had repeated his lie so often now, he almost believed it himself.

Amy, however, looked unconvinced. "So how come a music producer has delivery notes from Electrical Showstoppers in his motorbike?" she said.

Spencer stared at her. So she *had* seen the NanoDecs in the bike pannier.

"Don't worry, I'm not going to say anything." Amy smiled. "What does your dad *really* do – work for Electrical Showstoppers?"

Spencer's stomach flipped over. "I don't know what you're talking about," he said. "Why don't you mind your own business, fatso?"

There was a pause. Two red spots appeared on Amy's round cheeks. "You know, Spencer," she said. "I'm only trying to be your friend. But if you're too stupid to see that then maybe I just won't bother."

And, before Spencer could say anything, she stomped out of the classroom.

At first, Spencer was worried Amy might tell everyone what she'd seen. But as lunch break came and went, it was obvious she'd kept her promise not to say anything. Spencer relaxed into the rest of the day. He hung out with Kieran and his friends.

Kieran was really cool – into breaking all the stupid school rules whenever he could. Things like chewing gum and running in the corridors and playing in the broken-down shed in the corner of the playground.

By the time Spencer left school that afternoon, he felt he'd had the best second day at a new school ever.

And then he got home.

Dad was on his feet and in the corridor before Spencer had even fully opened the front door.

"Spencer, thank goodness you're back." Dad looked a right state, even for him. His hair was wild and standing out from his head. He was unshaven and dressed in a stained, torn T-shirt. Something twisted in Spencer's stomach. Dad hadn't looked this bad since just after Mum died.

"What's up?" he asked. But in his heart he already knew.

"A NanoDec I was supposed to deliver today wasn't in the box you took out of my bike last night." Dad ran his hands through his hair so it stuck out even more. "You've got to help me look for it, son. Seriously. The shop says that if I don't find it within 24 hours then I'll be fired."

"It can't have just vanished." Dad paced across the living room again. "I mean, it must be here somewhere."

Spencer sank further into the sofa. He'd already pretended to help Dad look for the NanoDec for most of the evening.

"Let's retrace your steps again, son."

"But we've already done that a million times." Spencer felt terrible. Worse than terrible. He knew he should just come clean to Dad about the NanoDec, but something held him back. Partly it was fear of Dad's anger. But mostly it was not being able to bear the idea of him knowing what he'd done. Because the worst thing, by far, was that Dad hadn't, not for a single second, done or said anything to suggest that Spencer might have taken the NanoDec deliberately.

"Come on, Spencer. Help." Dad turned over a cushion for the tenth time. "My job's on the line here."

Two hours later, at 11 o'clock, Dad told Spencer to go to bed. "We can try again in the morning. I've got 'til the shop closes tomorrow to find it."

"Can't you just buy a replacement?" Spencer said.

"With what?" Dad sighed. "I'm struggling to get this month's rent together as it is. If I lose my job, there's no way we'll make it..."

As Spencer got into bed, he knew that whatever it took, he was somehow going to have to get that NanoDec back off Kieran – and do it tomorrow.

Year 6 games had just started. Earlier, when Spencer had hinted he might need the NanoDec back, Kieran had just laughed. It was obvious he wasn't going to hand it over. Which left Spencer with only one option.

He kicked the ball around for a few minutes, then told the teacher, Mr Jeffs, he needed to go to the toilet. He raced down to the boys changing rooms, where he knew the NanoDec was safe inside Kieran's locker. So far, so good.

Panting, he found Kieran's locker – it wasn't hard, what with the huge black K painted over the chipped grey metal. He took Dad's plastic video club card, which he'd taken from the kitchen counter that morning, and started sliding the card up and down, trying to force the little metal catch back.

"I knew it." Amy's voice rang out, accusingly.

Spencer jumped. He spun round. Amy was right behind him, hands on her hips.

"You're trying to get that NanoDec back. I saw the box. You nicked it out of your dad's bike, didn't you?"

Spencer's heart pounded. "So?" he said.

"You admit you *stole* your dad's NanoDec?" Amy's eyes widened further.

"No. Well, yes." Spencer wanted to come up with a fantastic lie that would convince Amy he hadn't done anything wrong, but a) he couldn't think of one and b) one look at Amy's face told him there was no point in pretending any more.

"It wasn't my dad's NanoDec," he said. "I just took one he was supposed to be delivering the next day."

"I didn't *think* he was a music producer." Amy's eyes were practically circles.

"Well, you were right." Spencer turned back to Kieran's locker and started sliding the card up and down the slit again. "He's a motorbike courier."

"Why did you pretend that he—?"

"I don't know." Spencer stopped sliding the card. His hands were sweaty and it kept slipping. "Who d'you think you are, anyway, following me down here? Why don't you keep your fat, interfering nose out of it?"

There was silence behind him. He turned round. To his horror, Amy's eyes were full of tears. She blinked them back.

"I wish you'd never come to this school, Spencer Sykes," she said. "You're not worth trying to be friends with."

Spencer shuffled uncomfortably, the NanoDec temporarily forgotten. Maybe he had been mean. "I'm sorry," he said slowly. "I... I suppose I lied because at the time it seemed like the right thing to do. And then, when I got home and found my dad was actually delivering a bunch of NanoDecs, it was like... I dunno... like it was fate..."

Amy sniffed. "What, like the universe was *telling* you to steal one?" she said sarcastically.

"No." Spencer shrugged. "It just seemed like it was supposed to happen, but then... then my dad got in trouble at work over it and if I don't get that NanoDec back to him, he'll be fired."

"No way!" Amy gasped. "You can't let that happen."

"I know." Spencer turned back to Kieran's locker. "That's why I'm here."

Amy took the video club card out of his hand. "Here," she said. "There's a knack to it." With a single, swift swipe Amy pushed the card along the slit. The locker door swung open.

"Impressive." Spencer grinned.

Amy shrugged. "I'm going to be a mechanic when I'm older. Like my brother."

Spencer saw the NanoDec straightway – its shiny edge peeking out from behind a screwed-up bundle of school clothes. The charger and the bright-blue box it had come in were there, too. Spencer breathed a sigh of relief. He grabbed the NanoDec, shoved it into its packaging, then pushed the locker door shut.

"Quick," Amy said. "Someone's coming."

Spencer rammed the box into his school bag. He stepped away from the locker just as the doors swung open and Kieran ran in.

"Hi, Spencer," he grinned. "What're you doing here? Mr Jeffs sent me down to get the spare footballs." He caught sight of Amy. "Hey, fatso, just 'cos you look like a boy doesn't mean you can come into these changing rooms. Get out."

"I was just..." Amy began, but before she could finish her sentence Kieran swore.

"My locker's open!" He yanked at the door. "Someone's taken my NanoDec!" He glared at Amy. "Was it you, fatso?"

"No, it wasn't." Spencer said. "And don't call her that."

Kieran stared at him. "What did you say?"

"I think it was that boy who just left," Amy said quickly. "Spencer and I were passing on our way to the loos just as he was leaving. We only saw him from behind, but he was looking round – like, in this secretive way – then he ran off."

Kieran glanced at Spencer. "This true?"

Spencer nodded.

"What did he look like?"

"Skinny, sandy hair, jumper too big for him," Amy said.

Kieran stared at them both. "That sounds like Jamie Thurston in Year 5."

"I don't think it was..." Amy began.

"Wait 'til I find him." Kieran slammed his locker door shut, locked it, then turned to

Spencer. "Come on."

"But we don't know if it was him," Spencer said weakly.

"Sure we do," said Kieran.

Spencer glanced at Amy.

"*She's* not coming with us," Kieran snapped.

Amy rolled her eyes. "Don't worry. I don't want to." And she turned and stalked out of the changing room.

Spencer watched her go, feeling uncomfortable. Amy had just helped him find the NanoDec and cover up what he'd done. It seemed mean to let Kieran order her away.

"What are you doing, hanging round with *her* anyway?" Kieran demanded.

"I'm not," Spencer said. "We just happened to be down here at the same time."

"Right." Kieran walked to the door. "Come on. We'll get Jamie soon as school is over, OK?"

Spencer nodded, numbly, and followed. They went back up to games. Amy was there already, but whenever Spencer looked at her, she refused to meet his eyes.

Spencer spent the rest of the afternoon trying to talk Kieran out of going after Jamie Thurston.

But Kieran was determined. He went on and on about how they were going to waylay Jamie on his way home.

As the day wore on, Spencer started to wish he was hanging out with Amy, chatting about bikes or whatever. But Amy didn't look at him once. Anyway, Kieran had made it clear that if Spencer wanted to be friends with him, he couldn't be friends with Amy, too.

At last the final bell rang. Spencer followed Kieran outside, across the playground.

"There's Jamie." Kieran pointed to a skinny, sandy-haired boy standing by the school gate.

Spencer gulped. Jamie was at least a head shorter than either of them, and half as wide. Kieran would beat him to a pulp.

"But he's not wearing a jumper," he said desperately. "Remember, Amy said he had on a jumper too big for him."

"I thought you were there, too." Kieran frowned. "Anyway, he probably took the jumper off."

"We only saw him from the back. I don't think it was him."

"Course it was," Kieran said. "Jamie's always making out he's better than everyone. I bet he'd kill for a NanoDec."

Out of the corner of his eye, Spencer saw Amy watching them. "What are you going to do?"

"Beat Jamie up 'til he gives back the NanoDec," Kieran said matter-of-factly.

Spencer was sure Amy had heard. She took a step towards them. Suddenly, he knew that she was going to tell Kieran everything rather than let him hurt Jamie. And, just as suddenly, Spencer saw what he had to do.

"Come on," Kieran said. "Jamie's leaving."

"We can't..." Spencer stopped, unsure how to say it.

Kieran turned on him. "*What* is your problem?" he demanded. "I have a right to get back what's mine from that thief."

"It wasn't him," Spencer blurted out.

"What?" Kieran frowned. "How d'you know?"

Spencer's heart raced. "Because it was me."

"But you *gave* me the NanoDec."

"Yes, but it wasn't mine in the first place. I stole it off my dad. He's... he's not a music producer, he's a delivery man, a motorbike courier. And now he's going to be sacked if I don't get it back to him, so... so..."

"So you thought you could just nick it off me?" Kieran stared at him, clearly disgusted. "Well, you can't. It's mine now. Give it back."

Spencer shook his head. "Didn't you hear me? My dad'll get the sack if I don't give him the NanoDec."

"You total loser." Kieran shoved him in the chest.

Spencer stumbled back a step, then turned and walked away. He looked over his shoulder. Kieran was glaring at him, but made no move to follow.

When Spencer got home, Dad was outside, tinkering with his bike in the front yard. He looked up at Spencer and shook his head.

"I didn't find it," he said. "I'm sorry, son. I don't know what to do."

Spencer took his bag off his shoulder. "Its OK, Dad," he said. "I've got the NanoDec." He pulled the bright-blue box out of the bag.

Dad scrambled to his feet. "How did you get that?" He grabbed Spencer's shoulder. "Promise me on your mother's memory that you didn't steal this to replace the one I lost."

"No." Spencer blew out his breath. "Well, sort of... I took one out of your bike yesterday. It was for this guy at school. But I got it back today.

Here." He thrust the NanoDec into his dad's hands.

"What?" Dad stared at him. "What are you talking about?"

As Spencer explained, Dad's face grew horrified, then angrier and angrier. Spencer stopped speaking and waited for the explosion.

"Hi, you must be Spencer's dad." Amy had strolled up, unnoticed. She smiled at Dad, who stared back at her, clearly unable to take in her presence on top of what Spencer had just told him.

"Spencer just did a brave thing," Amy went on. "He did a bad thing first, taking the NanoDec to try and make friends, but then he owned up to it to this big bully. And now his life at school's going to be a misery, so whatever punishment you're thinking of giving him, it won't be as bad as what he's going to get there. And at least you'll be able to keep your job now, won't you?"

"Er... I... " Dad raised his eyebrows. "And you are?"

"This is Amy," Spencer said. "She's the first friend I made at school." He grinned hopefully at Amy.

Amy nodded.

Dad gazed at them both. "Right."

"Nice bike, Mr Sykes," Amy said. "My brother has a Kawasaki Z650 twin. He says classic Kawasakis are more reliable than classic Triumphs."

"Mmm." Dad's expression lightened a little. "Well, I don't know about that, they're only unreliable if you don't work on them." He hesitated. "I guess as you're Spencer's friend you should come inside. Have some juice or something while I get this NanoDec delivered." He turned to Spencer. "Though we still need to talk," he said firmly. "A long and very serious talk."

"Thanks, Mr Sykes." Amy smiled. "I'd love some juice. So when did you buy your bike...?"

Spencer followed Dad and Amy up the steps to the flat. As he walked through the front door he smiled. However Dad decided to punish him and whatever happened with Kieran and the class tomorrow, with a friend like Amy, he thought he'd probably be able to handle it just fine.

ONE MORE STEP
BY JULIA GREEN

Time is running out! Only six more weeks and we will be leaving Southfield Primary for ever. It's weird to think that we won't all be coming back in September, not any of us. Even our teacher, Mrs Ives, is leaving. She's having a baby. Each week she tells us how big the baby is, growing inside her: it's gone from the size of a walnut to 38 cms and the weight of a big bag of sugar! She tells us what it's doing: "It can suck its thumb now!" "It can kick!" This week she told us how the baby's skin changes from transparent and paper thin, to more like ours, but wrinkly.

We sit at our table, Molly, Zak and me (I'm Lara), and imagine Mrs Ives' baby listening in to everything that happens in our classroom, all the laughing and chattering and singing.

The tadpoles in the aquarium on the windowsill are changing, too. They've got arms and legs now, and this morning Zak put a rock in the corner of the tank, ready for when they need to climb out of the water to breathe the air. As soon as they are little frogs, we'll let them free in the school garden.

Everything is growing and changing.

"That's life," Mr Breeze says in Assembly. "Nothing stays the same. Think of your life as a journey. We're always moving on. That's how it should be."

Growing and Changing is our topic for this term. Now that SATs are out of the way, we've pinned fresh paper to the classroom walls ready for our new displays. There's space for the Pembroke Project (we go away for a whole week, to Pembrokeshire in Wales), and another for Our Memories, ready for the leavers' service on our last day.

On the blue paper next to the door, Mrs Ives has written the heading Moving On, in her lovely curly writing. That's for stuff about all the different schools people will be going to in September. We can write what we're looking forward to, and anything we are worried about.

The Reading Tree is looking a bit tatty: it's been there all year, but no one did much reading when we were practising for the SATs. Just this week, though, Molly and me each added new leaves. We've read everything in the Year 6 boxes, so Mrs Ives has started bringing in her own books for us. I've just finished *A Little Princess*, which was quite old fashioned but I really loved it! I'm going to read *I Capture the Castle* next. Molly read *Lucky Star*. Zak, who sits on our table and is our best friend-who-is-a-boy (NOT a boyfriend), reads books about things, like with facts. Right now he's reading a book called *Wild World*.

Molly, Zak and me will all be going to the same secondary school. At first, Molly's mum wanted her to go to the girls' school because she went there when she was our age, and she thought it would be good for Molly and *help her focus*, but we begged and pleaded and she gave in. The three of us have been best friends since we were four, in Reception. We know each other inside out.

In May, something weird happened. Well, not exactly weird: just that Molly started to grow. We've always looked the same, like twins even (long, straight, brown hair, hazel eyes), but since Molly shot up like a beanpole she looks older, suddenly. We measured ourselves as part of the growing and changing project, and Molly is now second tallest in Year 6!

Mrs Ives handed out new books today, for writing in. They are our Transition Books, which go up with us to the new schools, so "be extra neat and try your best," she said. "You want to show your best work to your new teachers, don't you?"

When we write our names in ink on the yellow covers, Zak is concentrating so hard on being neat he leaves out an e in his name.

"Never mind," Mrs Ives says.

But he does mind, I can tell. I help him squeeze a skinny e in between the *g* and the *r*. Zak is very clever and knows loads of things, but he still writes like a spider, even now. Some things don't change!

It's Invasion Day tomorrow! We've always called it that: the day when everyone goes up a class for the day, to try it out. All the tiny babies come to Reception class, and everyone else shunts up. It hits me then, properly: all the Year 5s will be coming in here, to our classroom, and there's nowhere else for us to go... except secondary school. So that's what happens: we go to try it out. Not that we can then turn round and say well, we didn't like it, so we won't go. There isn't any option, is there?

"Don't be negative," my mum says in the morning. "You'll be fine."

"That's a long face," Dad says at breakfast.

I've got that squirmy feeling in my tummy. I'm just *so* glad I'm going on the bus with Molly and Zak. When Molly comes round to collect me, I have to change clothes again (you don't wear uniform till you start properly) because Molly says you can't wear jeans. Zak's forgotten to bring a pencil case or any lunch. He hasn't brought a bag at all.

Molly leads the way into the huge hall, being tallest. We sit in a middle row, just in case there are questions and they pick on people at the front to answer. There's a small group of us from Southfields, so we sit together, and luckily no one asks anything difficult: the head teacher says some things and then some teachers talk a bit and then we have to get into groups, for lessons. They've already made the lists, so you can't choose your group. Luckily, Molly, Zak and me are put together.

"They won't be proper lessons," Zak says. "They do fun things, to get you thinking it's always like that. Otherwise it would put you off."

In Art, we have a lovely messy time with squeezy paint and Perspex plates and rollers, making monoprints. In PE, we can choose trampolining, football or yoga. Zak does trampolining, and gets the giggles when he sees Molly and me being cats in yoga. The day goes by quite fast. We don't do any Maths or English. At lunch, there are free cakes. Our last lesson is drama, in a special studio with no windows and proper lighting equipment.

No one gets lost, even though there are so many rooms and corridors. It's not a bit like Southfields. Southfields is a tiny village school. I know the name of every single person there. It's bound to be a shock, isn't it?

Before we go home, a lady gives us a list for the school uniform.

"Are you going to wear skirt or trousers?" I ask Molly, at the bus stop. You can choose, if you are a girl.

"Trousers," Molly says.

I nod. "Me too."

"That's sexist," Zak says. "It's not fair."

Molly laughs. "You wear a skirt, then!"

Zak pushes Molly and a teacher frowns. But the bus is coming, so we don't get into trouble.

They've let us out early, before the rest of the school.

"So we don't get crushed to death," Zak says, "in the mad rush. Or bullied on the bus."

"Don't be so negative," I say.

"Anyway, I'm going to ride my bike to school, in September," Zak says.

Molly links arms with me. "We'll go on the bus together," she says. "Don't worry, Lara. Together, we're invincible."

Invincible is a word Molly learned from me. I like new words, especially long ones. There are lots in *A Little Princess*.

Walking along the lane to Southfield Primary the next morning, I seem to notice every tiny thing: the cow parsley in the hedge, and the newsagent shop, and the cat on the wall and the barky dog we pass every day. The chestnut tree next to the playground has leaves like huge hands, and where the candle-flowers were in spring, I can see the places where the conkers will come, in the autumn. Only this autumn, we won't be there to see them.

Mrs Ives thinks her baby will be born on the 12th August. Year 6 are helping her with names. Molly suggests *Lara Molly*. Mrs Ives laughs. "What if it's a boy?"

"Izak Luke," Molly says, as if she's been thinking about that already. She has being looking at Luke rather a lot, recently.

Luke is sitting at the back of the coach, and we're at the front, so she has to turn round a lot. Luke's hair looks different, kind of spiked up at the front. We're on our way to Pembroke, for the Year 6 school trip. We're not allowed to phone home all week. It's good for us to be independent, Mr Breeze says. "All part of growing up."

After we get settled in the dormitory at the hostel (girls in one room, boys in the other) we go for a town walk with clipboards and have to find old buildings and things like that. In the evening we play rounders after supper, in the shadow of the castle. Molly doesn't want to play. She goes off on her own right to the edge of the field, and pretends she's fielding but really she's thinking about Luke. I know, even though she doesn't tell me. I feel a bit sad.

The next day we visit the famous lily pools. You walk along little wooden bridges over these huge lakes covered in lilies and it is very beautiful, like a pink carpet you could walk on, only it's just flowers, growing in water. The air hums with a million insects. Andrew Leaky falls in. He had his eyes shut, apparently. Mrs Ives lends him some spare clothes from her emergency bag. The shorts come down below his knees. We all laugh. We settle down with sketch books and pastels to draw the lilies, except that I draw the dragonflies instead.

"Typical!" Molly says, peering over.

We go to a big, sandy beach for lunch. We're only allowed to paddle in the sea up to our knees: "Health and Safety," Mr Breeze says, through gritted teeth. "I know, I know, you can all swim, you'd be perfectly safe, but rules are rules."

Mrs Ives goes to sleep in the sun. I imagine her baby, floating in the warm sunlight shining on Mrs Ives' tummy. She's only wearing a thin T-shirt and you can see where her tummy button sticks out.

Zak lies down next to me on the sand and pokes at sand hoppers with a stick to make them hop. "Did you know," he says, "that a dragonfly larva spends a whole year growing, underwater, and it's carnivorous and eats tadpoles? And then when it climbs up a reed or a lily stem and hatches out and dries its wings, it only lives for a day?"

"Thank you for that information," I say, in a pretend-sarcastic voice, "and for elucidating the life cycle of the dragonfly."

"Swallowed the dictionary, Lara?" Andrew Leaky says, as usual.

We write postcards to our mums and dads, even though we'll be home in two days. "I wish I could stay here for ever," I write. I don't really mean that, but I love it being so sunny, and all the space, and knowing everyone, and playing beach cricket, and the singing.

On Friday, I learn to abseil down a wall. Zak has to be my buddy because he's the same height and weight as me, more or less. Molly gets to go with Luke and she is in heaven. She stays there (heaven) all the way home on the coach, next to Luke in the back seat. We sing the first verse of the leavers' song: *One more step along the road we go...*

We're so tired out we're all silent by the time the coach gets us back to school. Our parents are amazed!

Molly sucks the end of her pen. "What have you written?"

I show her. We're writing down memories of our school lives, the journeys of our life, and I've written about being stung by a wasp in Reception. It's how me and Molly made friends: she was the only person who listened when I tried to explain I wasn't crying about missing my mum, but because I'd been stung!

"I don't remember it," Molly says. "Anyway, you can't read that out. It's not very uplifting."

"Mrs Ives says we can have bad things as well as good," Zak says. He's writing (like a spider crawling across the lines) about breaking his arm when he fell off the wall in Year 3.

"It's not a bad thing," I say. "It's how Molly and me got to be friends."

Molly shows me her piece when she's finished. It's about being chosen to be Michaelmas Mouse in the school play, and learning how to move and speak like a mouse. It's funny, the way the things we remember are so totally different. We practise reading out our memories with Mrs Ives, who gets all teary-eyed. Later, we make banners for all the different schools we'll be going to. It's surprising how many different ones there are. Some are private, some for just boys or girls, or for a religion, like Catholics. At the leavers' service we will stand under our new school banners, to show where we're all going. We paint them bright colours, to look cheerful, even if we don't feel like that inside.

Each of us brings in a photo of ourselves as babies, for a competition to guess who is who. Mrs Ives pins them up, with numbers next to them. It's funny how often people look exactly the same, except bigger and with more hair. Baby Zak is doing the same thing with his hands as he does now, when he's worried about something. Baby Mrs Ives and Mr Breeze are easy to guess because the photos are old fashioned. It's funny to think that we were all once tiny babies and now look! We're all growing and changing, but we're still the same, too, inside. That's what I think.

"All the cells in your body get renewed every seven years," Zak tells me. "So actually you're not the same at all."

Time seems to be speeding up, like sand running through the egg timer on Mrs Ives' desk. Only one more week to go.

The little church is packed for the leavers' service with parents and grandparents and friends, and all the children and grown-ups from our school, so there's standing room only by the time Mum and Dad arrive (they both had to go to work in the morning). I made Mum promise not to cry, but of course she does, as soon as we start singing.

Shalom, Shalom,
May peace be with you
Throughout your days
In all that you do...

One by one, we step forward to read our memories, to share our life journeys. We each take a pebble from the bowl Mrs Ives holds out, ready to place on the stone cairn on the mound of grass at the back of the school garden when we leave the church. It's like a little bit of us will still be here, even though we've moved on.

I look round at my friends, all the people I've been with for seven whole years of my life, and remember happy things and sad ones, too, like the girl who got sick in Year 5 and isn't here today...

There's a time to laugh, there's a time to cry,
A time for birth, when you say hello,
A time to turn and wave goodbye...

The smaller children sitting on the hard wooden seats get fidgety. A Year 1 boy spots a big spider and there's a little flurry of panic along his bench. The children sitting behind him laugh.

Molly and I give the big bundle of flowers to Mrs Ives, and she makes a little speech about how much she's loved teaching us all, this year. How special each of us is.

Molly's fingers find mine. We stay like that, fingers entwined, through Mr Breeze's speech. We each have to step forward and shake hands with him and he gives us a dictionary with our names in.

Zak gives me a big grin. "You don't need one of those, Lara!" he whispers.

There's a lump in my throat, so I can hardly sing.

One more step along the road we go
And it's from the old we travel to the new
Keep me travelling along with you...

The service is almost over. We gather together under our new school banners. Luke and Molly hold ours up high and lead the way out of the church. I walk next to Zak behind them, down the nave and past all the children, past the mums and dads and grannies and grandpas and dinner ladies and the school secretary and the caretaker, Mr Hobbs. We hold our heads high, like we've practised, and our hearts are full. Out we go, and the Year 5 children step forward to take our places at the front of the church, singing the last song.

You shall go out with joy...

Out we go, each clutching our pebble, out from the dark inside of the small stone church that's been there for hundreds of years, out into the bright sunlight. One more step.

ABOUT THE AUTHORS

Gus Grenfell
has had many jobs in his life, including being a building society director, a market researcher, a folk musician and a teacher. He and his wife Tessa also ran a smallholding in Yorkshire, raising cattle, sheep, goats, pigs, poultry – and six children. They now live on the Isle of Arran.

Gus has had many short stories and poems published, as well as an adult novel. His first novel for younger readers, *Woodenface* – a historic fantasy set in the seventeenth century – was published in 2007.

Born in 1953 in Warrington, Cheshire, **Alan Gibbons** has been writing full time for many years. He has won the Blue Peter Book Award and six other book prizes. He has been shortlisted twice each for the Carnegie Medal (with *The Edge* and *Shadow of the Minotaur*) and the Booktrust Teenage Prize (with *The Edge*, *Caught in the Crossfire* and *The Dark Beneath*). Alan's latest book is *Scared to Death*, the first novel in the **Hell's Underground** series. Alan visits 150 schools a year and his books are published in nineteen languages. Alan lives in Liverpool with his wife and four children. You can find out more by visiting Alan's website www.alangibbons.com.

Meg Harper
writes a variety of books, from the humorous **My Mum** series to her recent gripping fantasies, *Fur* and *Piper*. She works part-time as a writer as she also runs a youth theatre. She loves her varied life, including working as a visiting author in schools and libraries. She has just finished a thriller for teenagers and is hoping to write a funny fantasy series for 6–8 year olds. She's also writing a fictional blog for her character, Kate. Visit it at www.megharper.co.uk and say what you think should happen next!

Francis McCrickard
is from Cleator, West Cumbria, and is married with twin daughters and a son. He has taught at

secondary schools in Britain, Zambia and Malawi, worked in local radio, and at national level in the Youth Services.

Francis now works with young people at a retreat centre in Ilkley, West Yorkshire. His published works include *The Boy and the Book* and *The Dead Are Listening*. His short story 'Superdad' is published in the anthology *Like Father, Like Son?*. Work is in progress on *Whatever*, a contemporary story for young adults that centres on an abduction, and *The Glass Chalice*, a fast-moving adventure story with the unique setting of ninth-century Ireland and Egypt.

Sophie McKenzie

was born and brought up in London, where she still lives. An ex-journalist, Sophie now teaches creative writing but spends as much of the week as she can on her own stories.

Sophie's first novel, *Girl, Missing*, was a Richard & Judy children's books winner and won the Red House Children's Book Award, older readers category, in 2007. Since then she has had three books published; *Six Steps to a Girl* and its sequel *Three's A Crowd* – plus the thriller, *Blood Ties*.

Julia Green

lives in Bath (not *in the bath*, although there is a watery theme in many of her stories). She writes novels for teenagers (*Blue Moon*, *Baby Blue*, *Hunter's Heart*) and younger children (*Over the Edge*, *Taking Flight*, *Sephy's Story*, *Beowulf the Brave*). Her next book for teenagers is called *Breathing Underwater*. Her favourite place to write would be a sunny café with a sea view, with a notebook, a cappuccino and an almond croissant, but most of the time she makes do with a laptop in the attic. She has two sons, and two cats, who like to help with writing stories, mainly by walking across the keyboard. Or sitting on it.